# THE PROGRESS OF AN OBJECT IN MOTION

## Curtis Gillespie

COTEAU BOOKS

The epigraph is taken from *Notebooks 1935-1942* by Albert Camus, published in a 1991 Paragon edition. Reprinted with permission of the publisher, Alfred A. Knopf.

Edited by Geoffrey Ursell.
Cover painting, *Thin Air*, by Iris Hauser.
Cover and book design by Minal Kharkar.
Author photo by Corey Anderson.
Printed and bound in Canada.

The publisher gratefully acknowledges the financial assistance of the Saskatchewan Arts Board, the Canada Council for the Arts, the Department of Canadian Heritage, and the City of Regina Arts Commission, for its publishing program.

## CANADIAN CATALOGUING IN PUBLICATION DATA

Gillespie, Curtis, 1960-

The progress of an object in motion

ISBN 1-55050-119-4

I. Title.

PS8563.I4819I'76 1997    C813'.54    C97-920094-6
PR9199.3.G544P76 1997

COTEAU BOOKS
401-2206 Dewdney Avenue
Regina, Saskatchewan
Canada, S4R 1H3

Available in the U.S. from:
General Distrubition Services Inc.
85 River Rock Drive, Ste 202
Buffalo, NY 14207

*For my father, Gerry (1931-1992) and*

*my daughter, Jessica (b. 1995), who*

*never met, except in my heart.*

*There are days when the world lies, days when it tells the truth.*

*It is telling the truth this evening—with what sad and insistent beauty.*

—*Albert Camus*

# Contents

Badlands **1**

Guadalajara **17**

The Progress of an Object in Motion **33**

Outriders **57**

The Meat Locker **75**

There's a Russian Tanker Stuck in the Harbour **93**

The Q Ball **115**

Angle of Incidence **129**

Sunflowers **147**

Ambassador **161**

New Rope **175**

The Coffin **197**

▲▲▲▲▲▲

▲▲▲▲▲▲▲

# BADLANDS

When I was sixteen my father's younger brother was in jail, and my father and I used to visit him together. "No one," my father said on the drive there one time, "is all good or all bad. Don't forget that."

I was driving, having just gotten my license, and he kept his eyes fixed on the highway, No. 9 to Drumheller. It was a lonely tarmac line that went east like a bridge to the horizon. "Any man can change his life around," he went on.

I remember wondering if he'd forgotten that Carla, Ivan's fiancée, was in the backseat. If he'd forgotten, or if he just didn't care what she thought. We didn't know her too well, but well enough for my mother and father to think that Ivan could do better. They thought Carla was a whore. A real one. This was the first time, eight months after he'd been sent up, that Carla had come with us from Calgary to Drumheller to visit Ivan in jail.

"So don't say anything that might hurt him," my father concluded.

He took his eye off the road and sort of looked over my way, though he might have been trying to sneak a look back at Carla, who sniffed when he finished. I glanced at her in the mirror and she flipped some loose blonde curls back off her forehead and stared out at the prairie, which was taking on shape and depth now that the sun had come up. She lit a cigarette and ignored us.

"Okay?" my father said. He wanted somebody to say something.

I didn't answer because I figured he was talking to Carla, though I still wasn't sure why he would think that would need saying. Carla was Ivan's fiancée, after all. They had planned the wedding for two years May, right after he finished his time. Ivan was my favourite uncle, still is, and he had asked me to be his best man, though I would only be eighteen by the time of the wedding. Ivan was twenty-six and Carla couldn't have been more than a few years older than me.

In any case, I didn't have much to say to Ivan, hurtful or otherwise. What could I possibly have to say that would interest him? I'd come with Dad once every few weeks and had probably said a hundred words total, hellos and goodbyes included.

It was fully light when we passed through the badlands and pulled into Drumheller. The town lay in a valley, in a slash on the prairie, and, at the bottom of the hill, at the entrance to the town, there was a big concrete dinosaur, standing on its hind legs. It was green and there was red paint dripping off its fangs. There were no people on the streets. The only sign of life was a coyote that limped in front of us at a light and then disappeared into an abandoned grocery store. We had passed the jail on the way in, but Dad wanted to rent a motel room first, so that we would have a home base. Ivan had a day pass.

The lady at the Dine-O-Saur Café and Motel wrote up a check-in card. "Just one night?" she asked.

"We'll actually be checking out around five o'clock today," my father said.

The lady looked at us in turn. She had pins in her hair and deeply yellow-stained fingers. "I'm still going to have to charge you for a full night." Her voice was flat but strained, like she was making an effort to not give away what she was thinking.

"No problem!" Carla blurted out. She licked her lips, then tousled my hair. "Is it, boys?"

The motel lady stopped and looked at Carla, and my father took a deep breath, pursing his lips when he exhaled. I thought it was funny but didn't laugh.

"Your business is your business," the lady said. She looked at us again. "That'll be cash."

We headed to the jail, which was only five minutes back along the highway we'd come in on. It was a cold morning and even from the town you could see the plumes of steam rising from the stacks of the penitentiary grounds, though you couldn't see the jail proper because of the steep valley walls.

We always met Ivan at the Visitor Centre, but today, because of the day pass, we were to pick him up at the South Door. We waited for about ten minutes before he finally appeared with a guard. He wore his prison clothes but had a shopping bag with him. They stopped at some desk behind a half-wall, and spoke. Actually, all Ivan did was nod his head. He looked our way once but didn't express any kind of emotion other than a quick smile. We stood nervously waiting.

The guard came right up to us with him. "He's all yours for today."

"Thank you," my father said. "Thank you."

"My pleasure," the guard said. He stood there with arms folded across his chest and his hands in his armpits. "Less work for us, get these guys out of here for awhile."

"Do they ever let you fellas out?" Carla asked him.

"Don't, Carla," said Ivan. His voice was calm.

The guard looked at Carla, then Ivan, and he nodded slowly,

as if he were allowing something to register fully. Then he turned and walked back into the jail. We heard a door close and lock somewhere not too far away.

Ivan turned on Carla. "Do you know how hard it is to get a day pass? Don't fuck it up with your little attitude."

"I've missed you, too, Hon." She made a sarcastic face, but then softened and kissed Ivan. They hugged for a minute, then my father spoke.

"We got a room in town, Ivan. It'll be nice to catch up and chat somewhere other than here for a change."

"That's a fact," he said. He looked at me as if he'd seen me for the first time. "And how's Robby?"

"Fine," I said.

"We're all fine," said my father. "How about some breakfast?"

After breakfast we got our stuff out of the car and went up to the motel room. There still weren't many people in the streets. It was March, and so winter was running down, but it was a cold bright day and our breath leapt steaming out of our throats.

Inside the dingy little room were two double beds, and two chairs and a table. Carla turned on the TV as soon as we got in. "Might as well watch Donahue," she said, kicking off her running shoes and tossing her coat on the bed, where she then sat. "What are we gonna do all day? Talk?"

"That's what we usually do," my father said. He took off his coat and shoes, and hung the coat up behind the door. I did the same.

Ivan smiled at Carla, then looked over at us. "Pretty boring, eh, Carla. Maybe we can talk these two into going out for lunch on their own, then you and I can have our own visit."

Carla let out a cackle and my father pasted on the same smile he used at church. "Lunch," she said. "Yeah."

Ivan and my father sat in the chairs at the table, so I sat on the bed farthest from the TV. They talked about family things for the whole of the Donahue show. Carla didn't even pretend to be interested in the family news that my father had to pass on to Ivan. I listened to them but watched Carla. She was on her stomach facing the TV. Her jeans were riding up her legs, bunching up a little towards her behind.

We passed the whole of the morning that way, Carla watching TV, my father and uncle talking. Ivan seemed to feed off of him, hunching forward with every piece of interesting news, nodding a lot, smiling knowing smiles. He appeared so gentle, Ivan, it was hard to believe he would hurt another person. But he had.

I was sent at one point to get coffee and donuts for everybody. It was still cold but the streets had some life now. The people seemed like other people. I always expected to see obviously criminal people in Drumheller, but I never could tell if they were criminal or not. It never occurred to me that escapees would likely go somewhere else.

At noon my father said, "Robby. Why don't you and I go grab some lunch. We can bring something back for these two." He asked Ivan and Carla what they wanted, and said we would be about an hour. Carla was grinning the whole time we were putting on our shoes and coats. As we walked out the door Ivan said something under his breath that made her snort with laughter.

When we came back with the food, exactly an hour later, Ivan was watching the TV and Carla was in the shower. Ivan turned off the TV, took his burger and fries and started on it with obvious pleasure. He squirted ketchup all over the fries, and created a separate pool of ketchup into which he occasionally dipped his hamburger. I sat down on the bed nearer the door.

"Food," he said, "has taste out here. Inside, you turn off your senses. Everything shuts down, except how to survive."

"That bad?" my father asked.

"Everything," he said between mouthfuls, "is measured on only one scale. Will this get me out quicker and make my stay more bearable, or will it keep me here longer and make it tougher? That's it."

"You've got to find a way."

"You're right, Richard," he said. "It's hard, knowing what I'm missing." He nodded towards the bathroom. "Thanks."

"You miss that?" my father said. "Her?"

"Yes."

"I don't think I'd miss a whore," my father said.

Much to my surprise, Ivan did not get upset. He seemed to become patient with my father. "Don't be so hard on her. She's done bad things before, but who hasn't? She told me she only ever gave blow jobs, nothing worse. Is that so bad on the scale of things? What I did was worse."

"I don't think so."

After Ivan finished eating he turned to me. "How's your mother?"

"She's okay, I guess." I looked at him from the bed. He always asked me how she was, and had never asked my father. At the time I was aware there was a tension between Ivan and my mother. At family dinners, Christmas, Easter, it was Ivan who would argue with anybody. He was a smart guy, and what always seemed to bother my mother was that she didn't think Ivan believed in anything, that he just took any side of an argument so that he could provoke somebody. Usually teasing, sometimes not.

My mother was someone who staked out where she stood on any issue. She was careful, and she always complained to my father, who tried to stay out of it, that careful was exactly what Ivan was not. Him ending up in jail was proof, and made it easier for her to say that he didn't care about anything, though I didn't agree with her. I don't think my father did, either. My mother's problem was just that she took Ivan too seriously. Ivan was my favourite uncle and that scared her, which may have partly explained why he continued to be my favourite.

"Is she ever going to come visit me?" Ivan asked. He was still looking at me, though I knew the question wasn't directed at me. I looked at my father. He sat still and watched me answer.

"I don't know," I said. "Maybe."

"Why don't you write her," my father said. "And ask her to."

Ivan pulled on the skin under his chin. "I just might, one of these days."

"She'd read it," my father said.

"Or frame it," said Ivan.

They both laughed, so I did, too. Carla came out of the bathroom at that moment.

"What's so funny?" She had her jeans on but the top button was undone, and her shirt was tied in a loose knot under her breasts. She was rubbing a towel over her head. I was on the bed nearest the bathroom. I could smell the damp flowery scent that came out of the bathroom with her, and I could see how small her feet were. I was struck by her bare feet. Without shoes or socks, they looked small enough to hold in my hands.

Ivan looked over. "Nothing, Hon."

She instantly pouted. "Sure," she said. She sat down on the edge of the bed I was on and put the towel completely over her head.

Ivan got up and came over beside her. "Carla," he said gently. He rubbed the outline of her head through the towel. "It was something else we were laughing about. Not you. Really." He looked at me and had a strange look in his eyes, as if we all needed to be understanding for some reason. "We were laughing at nothing. At me. Really." He kissed the towel where he thought her mouth might be. We could hear a muffled giggle from inside.

"Good," she said, getting up and switching on the television to a soap opera. She ignored the food we'd gotten her. There seemed to be less tension between her and Ivan since Dad and I had gone for lunch. For obvious reasons, I supposed.

Carla finished drying her hair and then tucked her shirt in haphazardly. She sat on the edge of the bed near the TV and listened to Ivan and my father talk about whatever subject happened to come up. I never talked anyway but she wouldn't have known that, and every now and then she would look over at me as if she was expecting something from me. Once she caught me looking at her.

"Well," said Ivan after about an hour. "I need some fresh air. I want a walk. Around a real street. Now that will be a pleasure for me." He stood up and stretched. I started to get off the bed. "No," he said. "Just me and your Dad." I looked at Dad and he looked a little surprised himself.

"I had an hour with Carla alone," said Ivan. "Now I want an hour with my brother. Maybe you and I will do something alone next time, Robby."

Carla didn't seem bothered by it, so Ivan and my father put on their shoes and coats, Ivan making jokes the whole while about making a run for it. Then they left saying they'd be back in an hour.

I was left alone with Carla and that wasn't all bad. She was at least nice to look at, though there was something about her that wasn't quite right. She called to mind something that required delicate handling and had instead been roughly treated, like a bruised piece of fruit. Maybe that was part of her appeal to men, who like to hurt the things that are susceptible to being hurt. I didn't want to hurt her, but I didn't particularly like her either.

She pulled out a cigarette and sat on one of the double beds, her back against the wall, one leg up to her chest, the other straight out. I sat in a chair by the TV at the foot of the bed, holding the TV guide. The box was still on, still turned to a soap opera. I could see the screen okay, but the images were distorted because of the angle from where I sat.

"So," she said after a couple of minutes. "You like your Uncle Ivan? A lot?" She flashed out blue wisps of smoke between her teeth.

I shrugged and nodded. "Don't you?"

She took another drag, then stubbed it out. She leaned over to the far side of the bed, stretching to reach her purse on the bedside table. Her shirt had come untucked in the back and I saw white skin and her backbone snaking down into her jeans.

She rolled back over with her purse and pulled out a joint.

"I was going to share this with everybody, but your Dad would shit." She lit it up. "Your Dad's a fucking drag." She looked at me for a response and offered me the joint by holding it at arm's length. I shook my head no.

"Are you and Ivan going to get married?" I said.

She took a long drag on the joint and closed her eyes as she held the smoke in her lungs. When she exhaled she tipped her head back and just let it filter out with a deep groan. She dropped her head back to look at me.

"What do you care?"

"Well," I said. "I am supposed to be the best man." It was all I could think to say.

She laughed out loud. "You're cute," she said. She looked at me for a long time and had another drag on the joint. She didn't offer me any this time. "How old are you?"

"How old are you?" I asked back.

"Well," she said slowly. "You are old enough to drive." She stubbed out the joint after taking a last toke, and held the smoke for a moment before making an O with her lips and blowing it in a line right at me. "And I am, too. That's old enough. Isn't it?"

I could really smell the dope. I shifted in my seat.

Carla slid down a bit on the bed so that she wasn't sitting so upright, and she put one hand behind her head, letting the other rest on her stomach. "I came out with you and your Dad today so that I could call it off with your Uncle Ivan. I figured he'd take it better with some family around."

"What!"

"That's right. It was practically over anyway."

"But you promised him you'd marry him."

"I know. I feel bad. I want to still be friends with him, though. Do you think he'll still be friends with me?"

"But why?"

"I just can't wait for him to get out. That's all. That's a long time."

"He'll wait," I said.

"Like he has a choice."

"That's not fair, Carla," I said. "That's just not fair."

"I'm too young to wait. I can't." She paused for a minute but kept her eyes on me. "And I can't not have any sex for two years. Or once a month, anyway. That I cannot do. Might as well not get any."

"Well," I said. "Maybe he would understand. You know."

She fixed a peculiar gaze at me. "Think so?" She took her arm from behind her head and put it on her lap with her other hand. "Who do you think Ivan would let me fuck for the next two years?"

I stared at her for a minute. "You're a slut," I said.

"That's a bad thing to call someone, Robby." She stayed still for a moment. "And it's not true, either. That's a horrible thing to call me."

I didn't move or say anything, but she slipped off the bed onto her knees. She stayed there for a few seconds like she was praying. Then she took steps on her knees over to where I was. She stopped in front of me, without touching me. Her arms were dangling at her sides.

"Do you think," she said, lifting her hands to her breasts and nipples, which I could see through her shirt. "Do you think he'd let me fuck you for the next two years?" She put her hands on my kneecaps and squeezed, then sent her hands nearer, tracing the inseam of my jeans upwards, her thumbs digging hard towards where my cock was pressing hard against my zipper. "That'd be all right, wouldn't it?"

I said no, or at least tried to say it, and I tried to move my legs out of her hands, but her chest was between my knees. Her hands met in the middle and she rubbed against me with them, like she was kneading dough. One hand moved to my belt and fly, the other kept circling against me. I thought she might look up, but she didn't. She seemed to be concentrating, and then she had me in her mouth.

I straightened my legs out and slouched a bit in the chair. After I came she kept her head down and her body hunched over. I could feel her hot breath and I left my hands on her head, still clutching her blonde hair. Then she drew herself up again, so that she was on her knees facing me. She looked at me and asked me if I liked that. I didn't answer, just stared at her. I felt like I was going to start shaking.

"I knew you would," she said. "I could tell." She drew herself closer to me and I could smell my semen on her breath. She ran her hand through my hair, and then dropped it down and took me in her hand. I got hard again. "Let's do it. Come on, Robby. I want you to fuck me! Come on!"

I took her hand off me without looking.

"Come on," she said. She started to undo her shirt and checked her watch. "Those guys won't be back for half an hour."

I stood up. "No," I said. For some reason I wanted to put my shoes on.

Carla stood up. Her shirt was undone and she tried to press against me.

"Don't," I said. "No!" I tried to back up and hit the chair. My knees gave a little and I half-fell into the chair I had just risen out of. I looked off to avoid her stare and saw the table with Ivan's empty cigarette package on it.

"No?" she said, standing over me. She nodded and half-smiled. "I was right."

I looked up. "What?"

She didn't answer me at first so I kept looking at her.

"I told Ivan you wouldn't," she said.

I blinked at her.

"You're cute," she said. "It might have been fun to do it. But what you know is the square root of fuck-all."

She turned and did up her shirt. I sat for a minute and then did up my pants. I went to the door and put on my shoes and coat. I had no particular desire to go out into the cold, but I wanted to be away from her. She had lit up a cigarette and was watching me. She wasn't anxious in the least, didn't say anything, just seemed to be enjoying her cigarette. I left and wandered out into the town. The sun was still above the fence-like valley walls, but it seemed like the light of the day was already starting to fade, and it made the town seem more stuck in an ill-lit ditch than located in a striking valley in the badlands.

I tried to time it so that I would arrive back just after my father and Ivan returned, but I lost track. When I walked back into the room Ivan and my father stopped talking.

"Jesus," said Ivan. "He decided to come back."

My father put down his drink and made a steeple with his hands. "Nice of you to join us. We were thinking we might have to leave you here."

"With all the criminals," said Ivan. They both grinned, and I glanced over at Carla. Ivan followed my look. She was sprawled on the bed reading a magazine, paying no attention to us. Ivan looked back at me but kept the same easy smile on his face.

"Well," said my father. "I hate to say it, but now that our intrepid traveller has returned I think we must depart."

Ivan's face went long, but he tried to keep up his humour. "That's for sure," he said. "Never stay here after sundown. Trust me." He went over to the track bag my father had brought. "Time to pack my own little suitcase." He took out a balloon and a jar of Vaseline. My father reached into his wallet and pulled out a number of bills. Carla also reached into her back pocket and pried some money from it. They handed the bills to him and he went into the bathroom and returned a couple of minutes later with no money and no balloon.

"Okay," he said. "Let's do it. I can only take so much of this freedom stuff."

I sat in the back all the way to Calgary. I made Carla sit in the front because I didn't want her looking at the back of my head for two hours. We passed through the badlands in the gaunt light of dusk, and you could see the ancient formations, stark and barren, looking as if nothing had lived in them for millions of years. The massive ridges of sandstone carved out of the land looked like the ribs of the earth. I sat thinking about what had happened. How could Ivan tell Carla to do those things to me? What reason would she have had to say what she did if it wasn't true? Just to be cruel? To make me feel better for letting her do it? I don't know.

We had a letter from Ivan a couple of months later, in which he explained that he and Carla had broken it off by mutual agreement and that they were still friends. He didn't say when or how they had split up. Just that she didn't want to wait for and then marry a con.

I didn't go with my father the next time he visited Ivan, but I did the time after, and things didn't seem different to me. Every visit for the next two years I looked at Ivan to see if Carla was telling the truth.

I was still his best man. Four years after he got out he married a nutritionist and moved to Red Deer, where he has lived a peaceful life ever since. Seven years after his marriage he was my best man. And not since his jail time has Carla's name come up. He has not spoken about her and no one, not my father, not my mother, not me, has asked about her. I haven't returned to the badlands, either, even though they're so close. But I remember them well, the lunar terrain, so bleak, so deeply indifferent to me and my world. I remember that with great clarity.

▲▲▲▲▲▲▲

# GUADALAJARA

My younger brother became a priest in 1971, in Guadalajara, Mexico, when he was eleven years old and I was thirteen. This was not the precise moment of his ordination, of course, yet I know that what happened in Guadalajara led him to his vocation. He's never told me this, and I've never asked him directly if it were true, but I believe it to be so.

For the Christmas holiday our family had driven from Edmonton to Mexico City. We stopped in Guadalajara the day before Christmas, and right after getting settled went shopping for gifts. The market was about the most confusing place I'd ever been, a planet of commerce wedged into what looked like a sports coliseum no longer fit for the purpose, with four or five levels and innumerable rows of stalls on each level. Our mother instructed us explicitly not to wander, and we didn't much, but it still wasn't long before we'd become separated from her and our father. They were spending a long time haggling over an onyx chess set. Graham and I had our attention diverted by the sound of some noisy birds an aisle over, and when we came back our parents were gone.

Graham became frightened immediately, and I did, too, and we tried to make our way down the narrow aisle in the general direction we'd been heading before. There were people everywhere and the aisle was maybe five feet wide, flanked by rows of rickety booths selling every kind of merchandise available. Bright fabrics, coffee beans, piñatas. Vegetables, knives, spices. Squawking chickens. Crucifixes, candles, leather. We were surrounded by stalls. It seemed as if everything you would ever want or need was in that market, and yet we couldn't find who we were looking for. We had no idea where our parents had gone, or even what place they might think to look for us.

A booth owner came over when we stopped to get our bearings, and patted our heads as if we were friendly stray dogs. I saw no one our own age around.

"We're trying to find our mom and dad," I said to the man. He smiled and pointed towards a couple of different exits, obviously unaware of what our problem was.

I thought our parents might look for us where we'd come in, and that it would be easier to find that entrance from the outside rather than wading through the chaos inside, so we left the market and started along the wide sidewalk around the outer wall. Graham stuck close to me. There was an entrance every fifty or sixty yards and they all looked the same, each abundant with people, shoppers, hawkers set up by the doors, and beggars, most of them deformed or crippled in some way, with hands or caps or cups extended.

We stopped in front of one entrance and stood for a moment. Graham was looking around, but stayed behind me. It was a cloudless day, and the sun bore squarely on us, direct and fiercely hot in a way we were unaccustomed to even in summer back home. Graham had a fairer complexion than I did, and without a hat or shade he would suffer after not too long. We set off again. After awhile I wasn't sure if we'd even gone all the way around or not, and we stopped and sat down just off the sidewalk, under the meagre shade of a near-dead tree.

People streamed past, but left us alone, except for a beggar. He had stumps for legs and came scrabbling up the sidewalk towards us, muttering in a pitiable voice. He rattled a few peso coins around in a tin can. I held out my hands indicating no money. Graham did the same but also spoke to the man. "I'm sorry," he said. "I wish we had some money for you." The man stared at Graham. His eyes were cloudy, like they were coated in wax paper. He turned his head, spat freely on the sidewalk, and moved on. A few minutes later, not twenty yards from us, he barked aggressively at someone who'd refused him money.

"Let's go," I said, getting up. "We should keep going."

Graham stayed seated. "Where?" he said. "I don't want to get up unless we're going where Mom and Dad are."

I ignored him and he slowly rose. We were at one of the corner entrances of the market. Traffic was pulsing through the intersection. Across from us was a huge cathedral, with massive bronze doors and a spire groping into the hot blue sky.

Graham stood up. "Let's go there," he said, pointing to the church.

I looked at him. "The church?"

"Yeah," he said. "Mom and Dad'll go there for sure."

I figured Graham was right. Our father was not a particularly religious man, yet he respected our mother's intense Catholicism, agreeing to let her raise us in her faith. If our parents did explore the perimeter of the market, they, or at least our mother, would certainly gravitate to the church to pray for God's help in finding us.

A mass was in progress when we entered the church, so we sat on a couple of loose chairs in the cool shade of the narthex. I felt an air of respite within the church, a haven from the chaos of heat and population outside. We didn't understand a word of what was being said, but still knew which part of the mass it was when the priest lifted the Bible to his face and kissed it. The reading of the Gospel. I could feel Graham relax beside me. All the symbols were the same. An altar, a massive crucifix overhead, the sacristy, bowls of holy water at the entrance.

We watched the mass through to the end, and sat as people drifted out. A few stayed behind, kneeling and praying, for another ten or fifteen minutes, until gradually the church emptied leaving Graham and I as the last ones in the cavernous space. We stepped into the back row of pews and sat down. There seemed no reason to leave, no one was asking us to.

A priest, not the one who had just offered mass, but a much younger one, came out of a side door at the transept, and went to the shelf in the apse. He opened a cabinet under the crucifix and removed some communion wafers. He turned to go back through the transept door, when he looked out over the church and saw us in the back row.

He said something to us in Spanish, his voice like a deep horn sounding across the high empty space. We remained silent because there was little we could say. He repeated himself, then stepped off the bema and walked down the centre aisle. He took a seat in the pew beside us.

"We're lost," I said.

We didn't understand any of what he said next, so we sat looking at him. He shook his head slightly and smiled for us. His teeth were yellow and he had thick short hair that nearly touched his eyebrows at his temples. He silently motioned for us to follow him. Unthinkingly, automatically, we did so. The three of us walked down the centre aisle, up past the altar, and back out the transept door into a long and dark hallway that took us to a kind of classroom with makeshift pews and about five rows of chairs.

The same priest who'd just finished offering mass in the cathedral was speaking to a new congregation, made up of people not like Graham and I. A sour smell, like old sweat, dominated the room. Those in the front row of the congregation all seemed crippled in one way or another, many missing limbs. The other seats were filled with dirty and sad looking people. Some were muttering to themselves, not following what the priest was saying.

The young priest pointed to chairs along the side wall and we went and sat down. Nearly everybody turned to look at us. The other priest, who looked about our father's age and had a heavy beard, continued to offer mass, glancing our way now and then.

When it came time to deliver communion, rather than stand at the head of the aisle and receive communicants, the priest circulated amongst the group, perhaps forty strong, carrying the chalice, holding each wafer aloft while blessing it. Some of the congregation were blind, and they thrust out their tongues even though the priest was two or three people away. They just opened their mouths like baby robins and waited.

When he finished delivering communion, the priest transferred the remaining wafers into a shallow dish and set it aside. He poured red wine into the chalice, blessed and drank it. Then he meticulously cleaned the chalice, folded the cleansing napkin and carefully placed it over the chalice. While he was doing this the younger priest murmured in his ear. They glanced back to us.

After mass the congregation was slow to disperse and most of them made no move at all to leave. They merely sat, perhaps in reflection or just to relish a quiet moment before having to go back outside to meet the heat and the derision of the population. Both priests came over to where Graham and I sat.

The older priest stopped in front of us, the younger remained deferentially behind.

"Hello," he said in thickly accented English. "Father Hervé is my name." He bent over warily and put out his hand palm up.

"Hello," I said, placing my hand in his.

"Hi," said Graham, who discreetly grabbed onto my shirt.

Father Hervé turned to the other priest and back to us. "This is Father Michael." Father Michael said something in rapid Spanish. Father Hervé listened but kept his gaze on us, smiling the whole time. He nodded once or twice, then asked us our names. We told him.

"And you were in the mass before, then?" he said to us.

I nodded back. "We're lost," I said. "Not really lost, but we're lost from our mom and dad."

Graham was not looking at Father Hervé any more. He was watching the beggars and cripples, who were still sitting quietly in the makeshift pews. They were just talking amongst themselves. Three blind people sat together and they seemed to be waiting for something, for everyone else to leave perhaps. Their eyes looked milky and distant like those of the beggar who'd approached us on the street.

"Where did you get lost?" asked Father Hervé.

"At the market," I said. "But our mom and dad might come here to pray."

Father Hervé's smile broke through his beard. "Of course, they will find you. Father Michael and I will make sure of that. But let us first finish. With our people here." He waved his hand across the room. "Then we will look for your mother and father."

Graham pointed to the others in the room. "Why are they in here?" he asked. "Why weren't they at the other mass?" He looked back to Father Hervé.

The priest stood upright. "They have their own special mass."

"Why?"

"Graham." I gave him a little elbow in the ribs.

"They are extra special to God," said Father Hervé patiently. "We help them talk to Him."

Graham sat back in his chair. I could tell by the way he looked back at the people that he was fascinated. "Why are they so special to God?" he said.

"The Lord knows they need him more than the rest. Now, you wait a few moments more, then Father Michael and I will help find your parents." He smiled broadly for us. I liked him, and Graham seemed okay with him, too. He left and went back to the front of the congregation.

Father Hervé said something softly and the group circled their chairs so that the blind people did not have to move. Once they'd settled, the priests handed out a small Bible to each person, including the blind people. Father Michael said two or three words, and everyone opened the books to a certain page. The blind people held their Bibles in both hands, like plates of food, and sat still but attentive, almost sniffing the air.

Father Michael read from the Bible for about five minutes while Father Hervé sat and listened. The group followed along closely, though one person nodded continuously. Another kept up a low mesmerizing drone, a kind of chant.

When Father Michael stopped reading there was a minute or two of complete silence, except for the droning man, who looked up but kept on with his noise. I could hear car horns and the noise of the street from outside. Father Hervé asked the group a question, waited, and then appeared to answer his own question, explaining himself at length and using his hands to balance one side of his exposition with the other. Some in the group listened intently, others seemed not to be paying any attention at all.

This went on for about twenty minutes, with Father Michael doing the reading and Father Hervé leading the discussion, of which there was little. Through all this I sat quietly, thinking about being lost, of maybe never being found, of how worried our mother and father were at that moment and what they were going to do to us for becoming lost. I wasn't paying much attention to what was going on in the room, barely noticing the people through my worry, but Graham was sitting upright, eyes scanning the room. He kept looking at Father Hervé and then back to the group, staring at each person in turn. A few minutes later some closed their Bibles.

When Father Hervé paused, Graham, in a voice everybody could hear, said, "What are you talking about?"

The two priests looked our direction, as did most of the group.

"We go to church, too," said Graham. "We read the Bible sometimes with the other altar boys."

Father Hervé smiled at us. "We should have asked you to join us. You would have helped us to pray." He motioned to a space beside him.

Instantly Graham was up and pulling his chair towards the group. Father Hervé smiled when Graham did this, so I moved mine over, too. We pulled into the circle and patiently sat while Father Hervé introduced us to everyone else. Neither Graham nor I knew what he said, but we recognized our names. Some of the people greeted us with smiles, most ignored us. One of the blind people turned our direction but seemed to gaze at a spot over our heads. Father Hervé continued for about another five minutes, then closed his Bible.

People started to disperse. The blind people waited, sitting patiently while the others rearranged the chairs. When that was done somebody said something and the blind rose from their chairs. One of them, the man who'd been droning throughout the mass and prayer session, tapped his way over to where we were still sitting. Father Hervé watched him come toward us and then followed him over. The blind man wore tattered clothes, and was very dirty. He had a jagged gash about an inch long under his chin that looked like it should have had stitches a week before. He stopped in front of us and started to talk. We looked to Father Hervé.

"He says," said Father Hervé, with a patient but slightly exasperated look on his face, "that he feels a holy presence in the room."

The blind man let a hand reach out, probe the nothingness in front of him. Graham and I involuntarily backed into our chairs.

He started to talk even more quickly. Again we looked to Father Hervé.

"Don't mind him," he said. "He is a nice man. Aren't you, Osvaldo?" Father Hervé patted Osvaldo on the shoulder.

Graham stood. His full height brought him only to Osvaldo's chest. "My name's Graham," he said.

The blind man groped out toward the sound of the voice. Father Hervé made a small involuntary move with his shoulders, a slight call to readiness, but held off. Graham reached out, and put Osvaldo's hand in his. Osvaldo smiled and turned his blank stare to Father Hervé, spoke again at some length, his voice cracking. He was a large man with enormous feet, but he had a pronounced stoop and made me think of someone who might be a circus clown.

"He says he feels your strength," said Father Hervé. "But he is a flatterer. He says the same to me often, once a month at least." He let out a low chuckle. Father Michael, picking up Bibles from chairs, also laughed. He took a stack in each arm and left the room.

Osvaldo reached for Graham's hand and held it at the wrist, moving it up towards his face. He closed his eyes and ran the tips of Graham's fingers over his eyelids two, three times, letting them linger at the last brush. Graham's four small fingertips fit neatly into the man's closed eye sockets.

He held Graham's hand for a moment longer with his eyes closed. He released it and opened his eyes, fixing a look directly at Graham. Then he made a rigid almost fearful move of his eyes to me.

Suddenly he let out a hysterical noise, a hyena-like yelp. His voice filled the small room like an alarm, and Graham and I shrank from it. He kept repeating something over and over. He bent over, took Graham's hand and began hungrily kissing his fingertips, pointing to his own eyes.

"Gracias!" he exclaimed. "Gracias! Gracias!" He repeated this and another word over and over, dancing crazily around the room, picking up objects from tables, inspecting them closely before replacing them. He looked up and down the walls, out the window. Graham staggered behind him, half-following, looking very confused, briefly examining his own hands. The other two blind people stood motionless by the door, unexcited, patiently waiting for Osvaldo.

I turned to Father Hervé and must have had a stunned look on my face. He leaned over and whispered in my ear. "He is not blind."

I looked up at him.

"I heal this man once a month, approximately," Father Hervé continued. "He is a great pretender."

Finally Osvaldo stopped dancing around the room. He spoke to Father Hervé and kept pointing to Graham as he did.

"He says that you have performed a miracle, and have made his life worth living," Father Hervé translated with an air of bemusement. Graham stood there looking like a victim of shell-shock. "He called you little Jesus," said Father Hervé, laughing. He patted Graham on the shoulder. "Perhaps you are, but not with our friend here." He pointed at Osvaldo and motioned to the door with a look of mock-impatience on his face. "Adios, Osvaldo."

Osvaldo picked up his cane, a dark wooden walking stick, and strode from the room chattering. The two people waiting for him followed behind, tapping their canes, click, click, click, down the hall.

There was quiet for a moment. Graham wandered back to where I stood. I was going to tell him what Father Hervé had just told me, that Osvaldo was not blind, but Father Michael re-entered the room. He made some motions to Father Hervé and spoke again but in much less rapid terms than before. He seemed relieved. Our parents, Father Hervé then explained, had come to the church door, holding our pictures. They were sitting in the pews that moment. We left the room and travelled back along the dark corridor.

"Graham," I said in a whisper, as we walked. "That guy wasn't really blind. Father Hervé told me."

He looked at me, but I wasn't sure if what I'd said had registered.

"He wasn't blind," I said again. I know he heard me, but before he could say anything we came to the end of the hallway, and back out onto the transept.

Our mother came running up the centre aisle and met us beside the altar. She hugged us both. Our father came up, too, trailing behind at a more modest pace, but I could tell from his face he'd been crying.

"Oh, Graham," our mother said, bursting into tears. "Andrew." She hugged us so hard I couldn't get my own arms around her.

Still flush with relief, our mother began to chastize us for becoming lost. She didn't really blame one or the other of us, but perhaps because I was the older child, her immediate attention was on me. I said nothing, just did my best not to cry, failing. Graham began to cry, too. The two priests stood watching.

While our mother was speaking, our father, whose tongue never could explain his heart, remained stoic. But our mother was gifted with the ability to project personal injury, which she used on us.

"We might never have found you," she said, her cheeks and hands visibly shaking. "You might have died, the two of you." Her anger began to rise through her ebbing relief.

Graham and I stood like garden trolls, and just looked at our feet. Our father stood a step behind our mother.

"Don't you ever do that to me again," she said, her voice a hoarse whisper. "Do you understand?"

"But it was okay, mom," Graham said quietly, breaking a silence I think our mother expected us to keep. Her mouth tightened into a grim line across her face. "We were safe here," he continued.

I nodded and said, "Yeah."

She was quiet for a moment and seemed to be trying to control nausea. "It was not okay," she said, her voice quivering.

"Honest, mom," Graham said. "We were all right." He looked at Father Hervé, who smiled.

The colour of our mother's face changed to a mottled purple. She said, "No," and then without any kind of warning slapped Graham across the side of the head, not violently, but high on the cheekbone and the temple. He winced audibly and his eyes watered. I flinched and stepped backward.

Father Hervé immediately came forward, just one step. "Please," he said in his thick English. "Please, they did the right thing."

Our mother's eyes went big. Our father moved towards her, like he was going to grab her if she tried it again. But her eyes stayed round and then went opaque. She moved forward and surrounded Graham in her arms, rocking back and forth, kissing the top of his head. "Oh God," our mother said softly but urgently. "Oh God, I'm sorry, honey. Graham?"

Graham stood with his arms at his sides, his hands in little fists. It was then I saw our mother loved Graham more than me. He let her go on holding him, and only slowly returned her embrace. I stood watching her hold him.

My father put his hand on top of my head and smoothed my hair, ran his big coarse thumb across my cheek. Father Hervé was gone the next time I looked around. He must have retreated very silently. I didn't see him go and when I left the church I was sorry not to be able to say goodbye.

Graham has never spoken a word to me about the way our mother reacted that day. He just took it in, blended it into the makeup of his person. I don't know if it had anything directly to do with him entering the priesthood. Or even whether part of him believed he'd healed Osvaldo. Whatever it was, he was different after that day.

I am now thirty-six, Graham thirty-four. He says his love for God is stronger than ever. He had then and has now the capacity, the gift, for love, and he seems happy with the way he's chosen to use it. He and my mother no longer talk, for reasons neither seems able to explain to me. Their estrangement came on gradually, like something growing in a dark cellar, a damp mould that goes unnoticed for years and, once discovered, cannot then be easily removed.

My mother rarely asks me now how Graham is doing. The only context in which she mentions him is to tell me that she still attends mass at St Clements in north Edmonton, a place I have not been in twenty years. She goes there to pray for him, and to pray for herself. She kneels down in the rear pews, where we always sat as a family, and prays hard, prays that she'll find him again.

I think she tells me this only in the hope that I will pass word of her supplications on to Graham, which will in turn encourage him to make the opening move in their reconciliation. Yet though I talk to him regularly, I've never mentioned it. I have occasionally considered saying something, but, usually after not much deliberation, I decide not to. Far be it from me to interfere with the power of prayer.

▲▲▲▲▲▲

# THE PROGRESS OF
# AN OBJECT IN MOTION

▲▲▲▲▲▲▲

**O**n those occasions when Marion said or did something odd, she knew her friends would say amongst themselves that such things were probably due to the metal plate in her head. Though not yet truly close to her friends in Calgary, having lived in the city only three years, Marion did enjoy their company, but they knew nothing of psychiatry or neurosurgery (though neither did she, really), and so it must have seemed perfectly logical to them that having a metal plate in your head would do something to a person besides allowing them to poke a fork into the part where the plate was, which Marion did occasionally to amuse them.

"Oh, Jesus, Marion," her friend Rona used to say when they were attending university at York. "That must hurt like hell!"

"Not at all," she'd say. "Pour me another glass of wine!"

Rona had been Marion's best friend at York, and they had stayed close despite never having lived in the same place since. Rona phoned one April evening from Ottawa, where she worked as a linguistics professor at Carleton. "What are you doing for holidays this year?" she half-shouted into the phone. "Do you want to go on a holiday with me?"

Marion thought her friend sounded funny, drunk perhaps, or sad. "Are you okay, Rona?"

"Hey," she said. "Sure. I was just thinking, maybe, the West Coast."

"How's Eric?" asked Marion.

There was a short silence. "He's fine," Rona said, and paused again. "Do you want to go on a holiday with me or not?"

"Of course," said Marion. "Of course I do."

When she was a child her parents had always taken Marion on driving holidays around the less-travelled parts of Ontario, leaving the blight of Scarborough behind. Her mother and father still lived there, in a residence for dying people. But on their "treks," as her father had called them, they would usually turn north between Toronto and Ottawa. She was never quite sure where they were when they stopped, though she never once felt lost or scared. Where they stopped usually just happened to be the place her father tired of driving.

"Here we are," he would say and shut off the car. Her mom would get the tent out of the trunk.

"Here?" Marion would say. "Where is here?

"Here is where we are," he'd say, spinning around goofily like Julie Andrews in *The Sound of Music*, making them all laugh. "Isn't it great!?"

She missed her father's plain talent for living, which had diminished incrementally as he'd aged. He had such an ability to take pleasure from things. That was not common, Marion always thought. He loved a cup of coffee, tying his shoelaces, a big bowl of buttered popcorn. "You haven't had popcorn unless your hands are greasy when you're done," he'd say, licking his fingers.

He was a self-employed butcher and they took holidays pretty much when they pleased, often deciding on a whim to pile in the car, usually forgetting swimming trunks or toothbrushes. One time they got back from a week-long trip and found they'd forgotten to lock the house.

They always blithely enjoyed their holidays—life, in fact—until Marion fell ill at sixteen with migraine after migraine. The headaches lasted a year. Four days after her seventeenth birthday they found a tumour in her cerebrum, just touching the *corpus collosum*. Three weeks later the growth was removed and part of her skull went with it. That was twenty years ago. During summer holidays.

As an engineer with the Longbow Consulting Group, Marion had four weeks holidays every year and had spent the last three summers driving around the prairies by herself, going down back highways, staying in small towns in cheap motels, seeing whatever sights there were to see, which was often nothing. That was fine with her. As long as there was a pool hall or some place where the local people hung out. She liked to go to bars and just watch people whom she had never seen before and would never see again, spending hours trying to imagine what the composition of their lives was, what on earth made them happy, if they were. Many times she had actually asked people, right out of the blue like she was asking for a dance, what gave them the will to keep on living. How could they just stand there and play pool? Drinking beer. Eating pretzels. What was the joy in their lives? The meaning?

The stolid brown-faced folk usually smiled politely and ignored her, assuming she was drunk or loopy. Sometimes people answered. Once, in the Leduc Legion, a small older woman with a bulbous face replied earnestly.

"Well, dear," said the woman. "For me life is memory; remembering what was good, I mean. Something is good only if it remembers good. I never think about anything until after, you know. If it remembers good it was good. But that's just myself maybe, eh?"

Marion was touched by that. How sensible it was, how simple! She smiled back at the woman.

"How 'bout you, dear?" said the lady.

"Pardon me?"

"What keeps you going?"

Marion stammered, hummed and hawed. The lady waited like the Sphinx.

Holding an index finger to the tip of her nose, trying to remember her physics, Marion said finally, "A moving object will remain in motion in the absence of retrograde forces."

The lady inched away slightly in her chair. "Is that right?"

Alberta was not a place Marion ever thought she would live. She never dreamed as a girl about living in Calgary, she knew that much, though she could never quite remember where she had dreamt about living. London, Paris, New York? Paris, probably, she liked to think.

But now she loved Calgary, loved the mountains to the west as everyone else did, privately adored the flatness to the east, and especially she loved chinooks, the warm winds peculiar to Alberta that blew over the Rockies at completely unpredictable times during the year. Those windy days, usually in the winter, when the air would suddenly get warm, when she could feel the weather, were magical for her. Such a day felt so much like an open window. Or a beginning. Sometimes during a chinook she would walk up to the treeless top of Nose Hill Park and let the wind go all over her, flap her clothes, play with her hair. Depression was not a strong enough word for those days when a chinook was visiting the city and she had to work late. A chinook was no good at night. She had to be able to see the arch, the soft clean edge that divided grey from blue. She had to feel the scope of the system and see it over her. Otherwise, it was just wind. From her office window a chinook held no power.

Work, her "career," was a difficult thing for Marion. Anton, the chairman of Longbow, had brought her to Calgary with a nice job offer three years ago, all the way from Fort Simpson in the Northwest Territories. Marion had enjoyed the north, but accepted Anton's offer to get away from a trapper she'd accidentally encouraged. Before Fort Simpson she'd worked in Toronto, Halifax and Montreal. Each job lasted only a few years, despite, her bosses always emphasized, the excellence of her work. Every job ended over "personality conflicts."

Anton and Marion had met in university. He'd asked her out while they were both at York some fifteen years earlier, but she said no right away. Her flat-out rejection of him, because, she told him, he had hair growing out of his ears, immediately endeared her to him and they became friends and stayed in touch. For years thereafter he sent pictures of his kids at Christmas and, in the manner of spurned but good-natured ex-suitors, asked politely in his letters about her love life. Was she seeing anybody? Was there someone who had stolen her heart? No, she always wrote back pitilessly, there wasn't.

Marion's immediate supervisor at Longbow turned out to be a knuckle-dragger called Dirk. He didn't talk much to her. She knew instinctively that she made him uncomfortable, and he generally stopped by her office only to offer up burnished pearls of male wisdom. She silently endured him for a month. One day he came by and leaned against her door, made some gossipy remark about another male staff person and then said, "You can always tell a man by his fingernails and shoes."

As was always the case in such circumstances, the only conversational options Marion's brain offered her were ones bound to be badly received. Am I the only one in the world that can't help myself, she often wondered? Everyone else she knew seemed so polite, so in control. Marion looked quizzically at Dirk's nicely polished loafers and then tried to look at his hands. "What is it exactly that I'm being told by your fingernails and shoes?" she asked him.

Dirk shuffled uneasily for a moment, fingered the perfect knot in his tie. "Well," he said, sniffing. "What do you think?"

She looked at him as if she'd been asked to consider a calculus problem. "I would imagine that you're vain. Or shallow. One of the two, though probably both now that I think about it."

Dirk looked at her like she had two heads. "Jesus Christ," he said.

Marion got called into Anton's office for that one and eventually tendered an apology, written by Anton, to Dirk, who was forced by Anton to accept it. Dirk remained her supervisor, but it was to the point now, three years later, that he never spoke to her face-to-face, instead using E-mail and Voice Message.

Marion stayed in the job only out of a sense of allegiance to Anton, and because she didn't particularly have anything better to do. Getting a paycheque was nice, that was true. She loved books, reading them, owning them, even just holding them. She had a cat, Martin, to feed. And she had to buy scotch. Her little one-bedroom apartment in Kensington had become a field hospital for friends wounded in the Partnered World. Sylvia was a regular. So was Helen. And Jennifer. They came, drank together, sometimes had a cry, talked freely, and, it seemed to Marion, always ended up boozily saying things like, "Marion, you are so lucky to have your freedom," or, "Marion, you have something I wish I had so badly, a sense of self, of just yourself."

Marion kept a little 4x6 green card in her big shoulder bag, on which was a saying by Thomas Mann she'd read and appropriated as her own years ago. "Hell is portable," he'd said. Sometimes she was tempted to pull her card out and read it to her friends when they got that way, so wrapped up in their own bitterness. Hell is portable, she wanted to say to them. Take yours when you leave.

Marion made it on to the right plane when it connected in Calgary on the way from Ottawa to Vancouver, and she sat down beside

Rona. They hugged and laughed, got arranged, and were soon airborne with a scotch in their hands.

"This is so exciting," said Marion. "It's as if we're running away somewhere. Like we're really escaping."

Rona nodded, wrinkled her nose, and leaned towards Marion. "Eric made love to me last night like some kind of pervert gymnast or something. I think he wanted to remind me what I'd be missing if I go back to women." Rona had been gay when they were roommates in university, probably still was, Marion figured, though she never asked much about it then or now. Though not gay herself, Marion was always a bit hurt that Rona had never expressed an interest in her sexually. She would have said no, but it would have been flattering to be wanted.

Rona had decided a few years ago she wanted kids, so she married Eric. Marion found him tolerable, although he did actually believe that Rona needed only to have sex with the right guy in order to go straight. Eric fancied himself a bit of a stud until they found out six months ago he was impotent. He was still in therapy, and Rona was investigating sperm banks.

Marion pursed her lips, waiting for the pervert gymnast punch line. There wasn't one.

"It just made me kind of sad, actually," said Rona.

Marion held her drink in both hands. Rona looked out the window and then back at Marion, who smiled.

"But tell me," said Rona. "How's the head?"

Marion pulled on a few strands of her fine chestnut brown hair, then rapped a couple knuckles against her skull. "Still there!" she said.

"Good," said Rona. "No more growths?"

"No. In fact, they think the whole brain may have atrophied."

"And the complications?"

"Complications? Is that what they call them now?"

"You know what I mean. 'Aberrant behaviour.'"

"God, Rona, is that me? Aberrant? Isn't that an awful word."

"I don't know if you're aberrant." They laughed and Rona signalled the stewardess for another scotch. "I don't think you're aberrant."

They spent the first couple of days of their holiday walking around Vancouver, visiting Granville Island, UBC, Wreck Beach where Rona took her top off but Marion didn't. They did some shopping one morning and then spent the whole afternoon in Stanley Park, walking the sea wall and playing miniature golf, which Marion enjoyed greatly. They ate sushi and went to the top of Grouse Mountain.

On the third morning after they arrived they packed up again and left for Horseshoe Bay to take the ferry to the Sunshine Coast. Rona had heard from a friend that it was beautiful and that there were some lovely B&B's up through Gibsons and Sechelt. They were booked in along the Sunshine Coast for the next four days.

"Look at that!" said Rona once they were aboard the ferry *Queen of Puget Sound,* out of Horseshoe Bay, heading towards Gibsons where they would debark. She was leaning on the railings of the upper deck peering through binoculars, and didn't elaborate for Marion what it was she was looking at.

Marion took a deep breath of the moist sea air. The texture of it was so different from the dry Calgary air that made her apartment a minefield of static electricity. She often worried about the frights she gave her cat Martin. If she walked across a room and then touched him, there would be a spark that was almost visible. Poor Martin would leap as if released from a catapult and run behind the TV. But here, out on a ship, with the wind and sea spit on her face, she could feel the suppleness and moisture return to her skin and touch.

They landed in Gibsons and caught a cab to the B&B, a quaint two story place named Hockworthy House. At the door they were met by a tall pale woman who introduced herself as Katja. After settling in and having a nap, they woke up hungry and decided to explore the town. They first checked with Katja for suggestions.

"Are you familiar wis Gibsons?" asked Katja with a nice but queerly intense smile. She had a vaguely eastern European accent. Hungarian or Romanian, Marion decided. "Sis is where *Beachcombers* was shot," she continued, punctuating her statement with an admonishing gesture of the index finger, an unnaturally long and knobbly digit. "Bait and Tackle is on sa pier beside Molly's Reach. You don't miss it."

"Right," they said in unison. "Right, thanks." They left the kitchen and hurried for the door, starting to laugh as they went.

Katja said loudly after them, "And sa door is locked at midnight, ladies."

Once they were off walking down the street, Rona said, "What a woman!"

"I know," laughed Marion. "But who knew we were coming to such a shrine! *The Beachcombers!*"

Rona responded with a forced yawn.

The Bait and Tackle sat at the land end of the main pier. Gibsons, which looked to be a town of perhaps 2,000 people, was right on the water and backed up into the hills that rose abruptly from the coast. It was quaint and picturesque in a way that reminded Marion of the east coast, the buildings densely packed so close to the water.

Directly across the street from The Bait and Tackle, just as Katja had said, was Molly's Reach. The place where the swarthy Nick Adonodis and his mangy rival Relic, icons of Canadian TV, had hung out for so many years on the CBC payroll.

"Look!?" said Marion, pointing to it. "That's the place! It looks so different than it did on TV."

"Big deal," said Rona. "The show got cancelled for a reason, you know. Besides, Bruno Gerussi never did it for me. Too hairy."

"How about Molly?" asked Marion. "You know, in that cute little apron." She went across the pier before Rona could answer, and gazed in the window of Molly's Reach. Rona stayed where she was at the foot of the pier, working, Marion suspected, on a comeback.

"It's closed," said Marion, shouting across the distance of perhaps forty metres.

Rona waved Marion back. "Come on, come on! Honestly, Marion, who cares about a cheesy TV series. I'm going in. Let's go." She turned and went into the pub without waiting to see if Marion was following.

Marion turned back and peered inside Molly's Reach one more time. It looked totally abandoned, not just closed. There were no chairs anywhere and a window in the far corner had been smashed. This sight saddened Marion because it seemed such a cozy place on the show, so warm when there was a fierce coastal storm outside, the coffee always on, that bald policeman hanging around. It gave her a safe feeling when she watched the show, but Molly's Reach looked cold and wooden now.

Rona had already seated herself when Marion went in the pub, and had two bottles of beer. The Bait and Tackle was a dimly lit place, but the east wall of the pub was windows and patio doors that opened up to the Gibsons harbour. The sun was just starting to fall, and it dappled off the water and reflected up into the bar, creating a sort of warm shimmering effect inside.

"Grab a chair and look at that menu," said Rona. "I'm so hungry I could eat a house."

"Horse."

"Pardon?"

"It's horse."

Rona looked at Marion for a moment and then shook her head. She leaned in and gave Marion a half-lidded look. "Sometimes, Marion, I simply do not have a single clue what you're talking about."

There was one other person in the pub. He was sitting a couple of tables away. "You're so hungry," he said loudly, "you could eat a horse. That's what she meant. The saying is horse not house."

Marion leaned across the table and punched Rona on the arm. "See. You're the one who's wrong." She turned around in her chair to see who had spoken. He was about forty, wearing a plaid flannel shirt and a baseball cap with a small bottle opener attached to the bill.

"Thanks," said Marion.

"No problem," he said.

Rona was facing him from across their table. "Yeah," she said sarcastically. "Thanks."

He turned out both palms and then playfully held up his beer bottle to Rona. "Hey, sorry, darling," he said. "The beer makes me brave. Let me buy you one. An apology beer."

"We have some," said Rona. "Thanks anyway."

"You're passing up a pretty good offer, you know. I don't buy many people beer. Not even two fresh trout like you."

Marion made a face. "Trout?! Is that a compliment?" She and Rona laughed.

"I'm a fisherman." The man didn't seem at all self-conscious. "Anyway, you don't like trout?"

They were laughing as the waitress came over to see if they needed anything.

"Well, if you must know," said Rona, in a loud voice. "I believe we are being harassed by that gentleman over there."

The waitress clucked her tongue. "Not the first time he's done that. Would you like me to speak to the manager?"

Rona narrowed her eyes at the man and cocked her head. "I think that would be best."

The waitress walked over to the man's table and said something to him in a whisper. She left his table and went behind the counter. The man got up, came over and sat down at their table.

"I understand you girls have a complaint," he said. "What can I do to help?"

"I thought you said you were a fisherman," Marion said. Rona sat back in her chair and sipped her beer, smiling.

"No lie," he said. "Crab and lobster, mostly, but this is off-season. Water's too warm this far south. All them crustaceans head north for the summer. Lots of guys follow 'em, but I stay and run this place. What d'ya think?" He looked around the room.

"Nice enough, I suppose," said Rona.

He pointed to their beers. "C'mon. On the house." They nodded and he got up right away. Marion followed him with her gaze. When he was at the bar he picked up the phone and made a quick call.

"He's got a cute butt," said Rona.

"I knew it," said Marion. "Is that what this is going to be? I'm sleeping in my bed tonight, Rona. Besides, you're married for heaven's sake."

Rona squinted at Marion. "What's your problem? That's very unkind, Marion. And presumptuous. I think it's you he wants."

Marion noticed Rona had a little wet mark on her chin, like she'd dribbled some beer. "Me?"

"Why not?"

"Yes, it's obvious, Rona. You're absolutely right. It's me he's interested in."

The fisherman came back with the beer and sat down. "My name's Bruce, by the way." He held out a big hand, which Rona shook first. When Marion shook his hand she thought it looked and felt more like a professional's hand than a fisherman's. There were no callouses, no cracked nails, no rough skin. Then again, he had said it was off-season.

Bruce looked from Marion to Rona then back to Marion. He put on an extremely gentlemanly tone. "I hope you girls don't mind, but I have taken the liberty of calling a friend of mine. He was coming anyway, but I told him I was pouring free beer, and he said he'd be right here."

"Another fisherman?" suggested Marion.

Bruce smiled. He did have a nice crooked-tooth kind of smile. "Yeah, he is actually."

"You must not make that much money," said Rona, "if you buy every 'trout' that comes in here beer. Not to mention, this place is empty. I hope that's not a reflection on the food."

"I hope not, too," said Bruce. "I do most of the cooking."

"Then maybe you can recommend something, because if I don't eat soon I'm going to die." Rona suddenly downed her glass of beer. "And bring me a scotch, for God's sake!"

Marion had kept her eye on Bruce from the moment he'd sat back down, and she soon decided he wanted nothing to do with her and would greatly prefer she were not there. He'd surely sped his friend along only to enhance his odds for a private audience with Rona. Marion wasn't mad, not at Bruce, anyway, or afraid, or even worried about being bored; she just wanted to spend her time with Rona. That was the point of the holiday.

Bruce went off to the kitchen to start making them dinner, and while he was gone, the place started filling up. It was getting darker outside, and the silhouettes of boats could be seen drifting into the harbour. The water caught the falling sun and mirrored pink and silver before everything went dark outside. By the time Bruce got back with their meals the bar had filled up considerably. Some people were playing darts and others were shooting pool in the corner. Marion thought that this was exactly the kind of place she would want to come if she were travelling alone. She would find a seat against a wall and watch people, maybe talk to one or two if she got curious, which she surely would.

"Oooh, thank you," said Rona, when Bruce put grilled salmon steaks in front of them. "Guess we won't see any more of you tonight. Not with this crowd." She looked at him and let her eyelids droop while she smiled. Marion wanted to groan.

"Nobody really eats. They all just come here mostly to drink."

Marion and Rona started in on the delicate pink fish, and Bruce disappeared. Not five minutes after they finished he came back to the table with his friend. He was taller than Bruce but not as good-looking. He had long bushy sideburns and wore a hat with a motor oil logo on it. His name was Simon, and he acted pretty much towards Marion as she expected he would, focussing on her if Bruce was at the table. When Bruce had to attend to one thing or another, Simon would enter into some innocuous conversation with both Marion and Rona, but would revert back to Marion alone when Bruce returned. He was running interference for Bruce, was all he was doing, although at regular intervals, almost as a kind of punctuation, Simon would look at Marion's breasts and try to see down her blouse. When she got up to go to the bathroom he blatantly ogled her.

Around midnight Bruce took Rona up to dance. The bar was still crowded but the dance floor was starting to thin out. Most everybody else in the place looked to be settling into some pretty hard drinking.

"So," said Simon, leaning in close to Marion. "Tell me a secret. About yourself. Something a simple fisherman like me can understand?" He put his hand on her knee under the table. Marion reached under and removed it, noticing as she did so that his hand did seem rougher and coarser and knobbier than Bruce's hand. This authenticity did not increase his attractiveness.

"Well," she said, pausing. "I have a steel plate in my head."

He sat up straight in his chair. "Huh?"

"It's true." She picked up a fork lying on the table and held it right in front of his face. "I could jab this into my head if you wanted me to."

"Don't!" he said. "Jesus." His cheek started twitching.

Marion leaned in towards him. "I'll tell you another one," she said. He took a drink of beer and listened without looking at her, staring agitatedly at an ashtray. "I castrated a man once," she whispered, adding, "by accident, of course."

He sat back stiffly in his chair and looked at her with a knotted brow. Bruce and Rona came back to the table with their arms around one another. Rona was slouching as though she wanted Bruce to hold her up.

"We're just going to go for a little drive," said Rona, laughing softly. "We won't be long. Do you mind?"

Marion looked over at Simon and then stood up. "I'm coming with you."

They piled into Bruce's truck, and he chattered about something for a few minutes. Marion was not listening to him and stared out the window. Rona poked her in the ribs.

"Preacher's Rock," she said. "That's where we're going, Marion!"

"A beautiful spot," Bruce continued. "As long as there aren't too many damn kids out there. It's a great big fucking rock that goes right out into the ocean. You can see it from the ferry, you know."

"Yes!" said Rona. "I saw it. With the binoculars." She turned to Marion, but Marion was staring out the window into the darkness. Rona took one hand off her purse and slipped it over onto Marion's lap and took hold of one of her hands. Marion squeezed back a little.

"If we get our courage up we can jump off!" Bruce guffawed. Suddenly he slammed on the brakes and they swayed forward in their seats. "Fuck," he said. "Sorry about that. I always miss the path." He grabbed a blanket from behind the seat and got out of the truck.

There were no signs or even visible paths, but Bruce led them to a narrow opening in the heavy scrub that bordered the road. After they'd been walking for a couple of minutes they came upon a small clearing in the bush. Seated around a small fire were a group of young people. The smell of dope hung heavy and sweet in the air.

"Hey!" said the group. There were four or five guys, a few girls, all teenagers. "Headed to the Rock?"

"Yes," said Rona. "Heard it's beautiful. We might even jump."

"Go for it," said one of them. A few of them snickered and made scary sounding noises. "Ooooh, I don't know, man," said one. "Long fuckin' way down."

"You pussy," said another, snorting. "It's a piece of cake. Did it yesterday." He reached over to a friend and took a joint.

Bruce and Rona pushed on, and though she thought for a moment she might prefer the company of these kids, Marion pushed on, also. When they got through the scrub they came out onto a flat expanse of rock that went for thirty or forty feet before dropping off straight into the ocean. The night was clear and perfect, and the moon lit up the whole plateau. They were the only ones out.

"Over there," said Bruce, pointing to the edge. "There's a great little place over there. You can sit on a ledge, like. It's a great place to come for, you know, a picnic, I guess." He winked at Rona.

"I'm a real third wheel here, aren't I?" Marion said glumly. "Why don't you two just go do your little thing somewhere and get it over with."

"Well, if you're going to pout, why don't you just join us," said Bruce. "I can handle the two of you girls, I think." He laughed, snickering sharply.

"I don't think so, buddy," said Rona, laughing, too. "You stay away from her."

Marion said, "My God, Rona. You're drunk. I mean, what on earth are you doing? You're about to have sex with a primate."

Rona laughed again, more softly, and came up to Marion. "Relax. Here, let me help you." Bruce instantly stripped, first pulling two rubbers from his pocket. Rona started undressing Marion.

"No!" Marion said. She shrugged Rona's arms off her.

Rona stopped and stood for a second. "Sorry," she said softly. "I mean..."

Marion walked around Rona, nearer to the edge of the rock. She could see just over the lip. The surface of the water wasn't visible. She looked out and tried hard to want what Rona wanted. What did Rona want? Was it anything she could want, too?

A loneliness she seemed to know suddenly dropped over her like a heavy canvas tent. It had an odour, old, wet, a little bit mouldy. She stood for a moment, looking out over the water. Lights blinked on the far shore of the bay. Marion took off her shirt and bra to see if it made anything feel different. She tossed them over her shoulder onto the ground where Bruce had dropped the blanket. It was a windless night and all that felt different being topless was less weight on her shoulders. She took off her pants and underwear, and flung them over by her other clothes. She was still facing the sea and hadn't looked back to where Bruce and Rona were.

"Marion?"

She turned around. Rona was standing about ten feet from her, Bruce fifteen. He was completely naked, but was starting to look really anxious about something, as if he suddenly might not be up to whatever was coming next. He had an erection, Marion could see that from where she stood in the dark. She looked at him briefly and turned back to look out over the water. She thought she might cry.

There was an almost unnatural stillness about this place. She could hear the sound of Rona's bare feet padding over to her across the smooth rock, and she thought she could even hear the sound of the tide gently slapping against the bottom of the cliff, however far down that was.

Rona came right up to Marion, and embraced her from behind, wrapping her arms around Marion's waist and resting her head on Marion's shoulder .

A little jolt ran up Marion's spine and across her scalp. She turned around and they hugged. Rona's skin was so soft, so warm. Marion had seen Rona naked in the gym locker room before, but had never really paid much attention. Marion wanted to keep hugging. She shivered but could feel her ears get hot. Rona lifted her face. They hugged for a few seconds longer and Rona let go, tracing a finger along Marion's collarbone.

"Hey!" said Bruce in a strained whisper from where he stood. "Is she joining us, or what?"

"We won't be too long," Rona said softly to Marion, so that Bruce wouldn't hear. "You're my sister, Marion. You are."

"Rona, darlin', grab the blanket," Bruce said in a louder, vaguely impatient way.

Rona picked up the blanket and walked off with Bruce into the scrub between the rock and the road. Marion's first thought was to hope that they would go far enough away so that she couldn't hear them. Her heart was pounding. She wanted to think about something else. She didn't want to think about what Rona and Bruce were going to do.

She turned and went over to the little perch Bruce had pointed to earlier. The air temperature was so perfectly comfortable, almost womb-like; warm but not hot, cool but not cold. At least Marion thought that a womb must feel like this. She sat down. This rock was a serene and naturally splendid spot. How sad, she thought, that her parents never got out to the west coast, to all this beauty. They'd never even gotten as far as Manitoba and never would now, stuck back in Scarborough in an old folk's home.

Looking up into the night, Marion saw stars everywhere. Millions of them. There were almost more stars than darkness. It suddenly occurred to her that she didn't know many of them, or even how to locate the ones she had seen before. She remembered some names. Venus? Artemis? Were these ones she should know? What about The Big Dipper? That was one she had definitely seen before, but not since she was a child. She searched the night sky for it and eventually gave up because her neck hurt. She bent her head toward the water. The actual surface couldn't be seen. How far was the drop? Twenty feet? Sixty? It was impossible to tell. She picked up a stone and dropped it into the darkness. One. Two. Three. Four. Five. Then a faint splash.

That seemed like a long way. She stood up, looked out and down. To dive, or, more precisely, to jump. What if she did? It was safe after all, hadn't those kids said so? Then again, they had been smoking dope.

She'd been off the high board at the pool when she was a kid. That was not so hard, though her mother had been standing on the edge with a life preserver. A count of five? That seemed about how far it was from off the high board. But did those kids mean safe at high tide or low tide? Of course, whatever they meant, Marion realized she had no idea whether the tide was in or out. And what if there were logs just under the surface of the water? Or if the rock wall swept out and under, with sharp jutting bits? But it was safe, it had to be, because even Bruce said they might jump off. Rona wouldn't hesitate. She would jump.

Marion stood up and got close to the edge. Her toes wiggled out an inch, then another. She only wished she knew how far a drop it was. Looking down, there was blackness and the sound of that lapping. Why not? she asked herself. Really. Why not? She wiggled out a bit further, the balls of her feet on rock and her toes out over nothing. She bent a little at the waist, then stood up. She looked out, not down, ahead, not below. She pushed her arms out in front of her to test the air for resistance, but there wasn't any. Nothing held her back. It was physics, plain and simple. She felt her knees bend and her ankles give, she felt her arms and legs go out.

YESSSSSSSS! She was in the air, screaming, screaming, but she managed to count, too, that was the amazing thing, she could count in her head even though she was shrieking for everything she was worth, yelling and whooping, yet counting as she fell.

One.

Two.

Three.

Four.

There was a slap and she disappeared. Stopped counting. The starry night vanished into a suffocating darkness and clouds filled her vision. Suddenly her eyes stung and she wanted to cry. She was cold, freezing, bitterly cold but that didn't last more than a second. There was no air for her to breathe and she knew that meant she was still under water. She closed her eyes and waited to come up, but it took longer than she thought it would, so that when she finally burst through the surface she had to gasp and gnash and swallow the air whole, chew at every little bit she could.

She treaded water and tried to orient herself. She turned to face the rock and looked up. The top was not there. The rock curved slightly away as it rose so that where she had leapt from was out of sight.

Suddenly she heard Rona's voice from above, screaming in terror. "MARION! OH, GOD, I'M SORRY! MARION! NO!"

She tried to shout up but got a briny mouthful of water and started coughing. She wasn't sure if Rona had heard her try to call or not, but she heard Rona keep on shouting, hysterically, although now it sounded as though she might be moving away from the edge, perhaps to find Bruce. Marion decided to get out right away, and crawl back up. She was vibrating up and down her body, the excitement and adrenaline still pumping through her. She paddled up to the wall of rock and as she was doing so noticed little lights everywhere in the water. They surrounded her like a thousand little water fairies, dancing and tickling, enveloping her like some kind of membrane. Suddenly she felt as though this aura had been assigned to her, like she'd been chosen for something special. This is my reward, she thought, a treat for having the courage to jump.

Marion got to the rock and found the face smooth and shiny. There were no footholds to help her climb out. It was sheer and slick, which she hadn't expected. Her arms started to ache from treading water.

Rona's voice echoed out again from above, sounding even further away and terribly sad, as if already resigned to something.

"I'm down here," said Marion as loudly as she could. "Down here." She let the words linger in the air for a minute, hoping Rona might catch them. There was no response.

Marion looked around as she treaded water. Now she could see the little waves slapping up against the sheer face of the rock wall. She could really feel her arms, especially in the forearms. Her thighs were starting to feel tight. There was no change in the rockface to her left, so she started to paddle to her right where it looked a bit craggier. She swam for twenty yards or so. The lights in the water followed her, playing all over her body. It was lovely, but she wished she was in a different circumstance so she could better enjoy the sensation. Fear touched her suddenly when she got to the craggy part and found the rock face had holds of sorts but that they progressed only five feet up the face before the rock went smooth again. At least she had a place to hold on and rest for a minute, which she did. She didn't have to swim or tread water, and as she rested the sound of Rona's voice came tumbling off the cliff, clearly receding in volume. Marion could not make out the words.

She felt better and less tired in her limbs now. She decided to put all her energy into one good long sustained yell. She belted out Rona's name as loud as she could for as long as she could. The only thing she got back was silence. Her fingers started to cramp from holding the rock tight, so she slipped back into the water and treaded for a minute. The ocean was warm and velvety on her skin and she felt wonderful without a suit on. So free, somehow, though she knew she was thinking stupid thoughts, treading water in the ocean with no idea how to get out. But a strange sort of calmness filled her. Bruce was a fisherman. There were boats. She would just hold on and yell occasionally, and everything would work out.

She felt her legs complain again, so she moved back towards the rockface. She watched the little pinpricks of light follow her hands until they cut through the surface of the water. She took hold of the same little nose of rock as before, and noticed the water level was an inch or two higher now. Or was it? She twisted her torso slightly and looked up.

The stars were still out. She thought for a moment she saw the Big Dipper. Right over there...but then, no, because, there, that was it, yes, right along there! Yes, it had to be! She stared at the elegant design, marvelling, so pleased with her accidental sighting. It was beautiful, and so obvious now that she'd found it in the sky.

There was a sort of handle, made up of a few stars, and a large ladle section, which was comprised of another five or six stars. Amazingly enough, Marion thought, all together they did look just like a big dipper. She laughed and kept staring, and laughed so giddily she began to feel lightheaded. The Big Dipper. It was huge, pinned up against the night like a dragonfly on a corkboard.

So huge, Marion suddenly thought, that if the Dipper wanted to, or if she could somehow make it do so, it could just come down from the sky and scoop all the water out of the sea. Just like that. Then she would be safe.

She secured her hold on the rockface with one hand and with the other reached out into the sky. Only when she saw the handle of the constellation was not within her reach did she draw her arm back to earth. Once again she held on to the rock with both hands, resting, looking up, admiring her discovery.

▲▲▲▲▲▲▲

# OUTRIDERS

▲▲▲▲▲▲▲

The Ponoka rodeo grounds were set up so that all the partici-
pants got paddock, trailer and wagon space out in the farmer's
field to the south and west of the track and fairground. It was
like a huge sprawled-out campground. Leroy's camp was on the
side opposite ours, but when Tommy and I went looking for it
that night, slinking around like thieves with all the other camps
dark, we got there soon enough.

Stealth was crucial. Leroy had been known to train his rifle
on animal, mineral or vegetable, depending on his mood and
degree of sobriety. I had once seen Leroy shoot a cat dead just
because it was spooking his horses. He shot it in the head with a
.22 and left it there, and the horses eventually mashed it into the
dirt.

"Gordo," said Tommy quietly. "Hey, Gordo."

"What," I said. The darkness was like the inside of a church
at night; the moon was glowing, and Leroy's Winnebago, parked
about twenty paces on the other side of his wagon, was as dark
and still as a sleeping elephant.

"Gordo," said Tommy. "You want to know what I'm thinking?" He put his peach-fuzz face near mine. His breath was hoarse and beery.

"What?"

"I think," he said, "that it was Leroy who did it. I really do."

For some reason we were both crouching like we badly needed a leak.

"Look here," Tommy continued. He pointed to something behind Leroy's stove-rack, the place at the back end of the chuckwagon where there should have been nothing but boards and dust and a tent pole or two. I couldn't see what he was pointing at. "Hang on," he said. He climbed up on the rig, silently, which surprised me because Tommy was always so clumsy. I couldn't tell what he was doing; there were shuffling sounds and then a grunt. He came out of the wagon and landed with a "poof."

"I told you," he said.

"What," I said. "What?"

"Shhh," he said. "Extra weight. Lots of it. I couldn't budge it. Like a chest or something."

"So what?"

"For somebody who's always telling me how smart he is," said Tommy, "you aren't going too far towards convincing me."

I surprised him with a couple of knuckles to the ribs. In one motion he open-handed me across the side of the head, knocking my hat off. "Stop it, you asshole," he said between his teeth. "You want Leroy out here?"

"Well, tell me what you're thinking, then."

"Figure it out. Why would Leroy carry all that weight? Must be four or five hundred pounds. He'd never win a race with a load like that."

"No, he wouldn't, would he?"

"But," said Tommy, "wouldn't you carry extra if you thought something might happen like what happened today?"

What had happened was a wagon pile-up. Both my step-father,

Dalton, and Leroy were in the race. Dalton had come out of the barrels in front. Two other teams were outside of him and closing when, for no reason I could see, one of the outside teams ran straight left into Dalton's horses. Tommy and I weren't far behind it all, following as outriders, whose job is to follow the wagon as a team. All Tommy and I had time to see was horses collide and wagons pile. Leroy stayed two or three lengths behind , and when everybody else piled he just swung wide and missed all of it. He coasted to the finish line and waved his hat to the silent crowd when he crossed.

A wagon pile-up is bad enough if you're watching, but you can't know what a piece of work it is unless you've been in one. Dalton was lucky to be still breathing, thrown like that from his seat under all those horses. Same with the other guys. We lost a couple horses, too, along with three from the other teams. Those sorry animals were on their backs scrabbling around, kicking one another, snorting, pawing, wide-eyed with panic, sensing they were as good as dead. It was difficult to tell which horse part belonged to which body. Three had to be destroyed, and two died instantly, one of them a horse named Alberta that was Dalton's favourite. She died when another wagon's wheel went over her neck and snapped it.

"Jesus, Tommy," I said, pointing to where the weight was at the back end of the Leroy's rig. "Are you sure he isn't just storing some stuff there between rides?" I looked over to Leroy's Winnebago, which was still dark.

"Maybe," said Tommy. "Maybe not."

"Jesus," I said. "The bastard."

The only reason we went skulking around Leroy's wagon in the first place was that we didn't like him. Other drivers on the wagon circuit didn't particularly like Leroy, but nobody hated him the way my stepfather Dalton did. Every time I came home from university, where I studied Agriculture, Dalton would have a Leroy Dank story to tell me.

Leroy had a reputation on the wagon circuit of being pretty shrewd with horseflesh, though not always above board. Dalton thought he'd been rooked a couple of times by Leroy, buying horses that got sick or went lame a few weeks later. He was convinced Leroy had done it on purpose, though he never proved any of it.

The morning after Tommy and I found that weight in Leroy's wagon, Dalton came up behind me in the paddock. I still wasn't quite sober from the night before and was fiddling around with the water hose, letting the horses get close to the trough and then jetting them flush on the side of the head. They would jump back and half circle until they would decide, always wrongly, that I could be trusted this time.

"Goddamit, Gordie!" Dalton yelled. "Stop queerin' them horses out!"

"Yessir." I held on to the hose but directed it at the ground by my feet.

"Tommy was tellin' me you think Leroy had something to do with that accident yesterday."

"What!" I said. "He said I thought that?"

"He said to ask you about it because he wasn't clear what you were on about."

Tommy was a coward. I would remind him of that later.

"Well," I said, "I'll tell you, but it wasn't me who came up with it." I pinched the hose and turned it back into the trough, making the water bubble.

Dalton said nothing, only stared at me. I told him what I knew.

"So you figure he set up that spill," Dalton said. "And took on the weight to stay behind, slow and steady."

That sounded possible, though I had no idea how Leroy could have set something like that up. "Sure," I said. "Why else is he going to lug five hundred pounds around a track?"

"Yeah," said Dalton. "Yeah, there's something awful strange about that." He took off his hat while he talked to me and ran a hand through his black hair. His hands were dirty, with chewed fingernails. They were big, too; one of them could easily go around my neck. He put his hat back on with all his hair under it. "Has Raymond heard about this?"

I shook my head no.

Raymond was the guy from the Society for the Prevention of Cruelty to Animals. That's how we knew him. As the guy from the SPCA. He was a guy the boys would have a beer with, but whenever there was a problem with the animals he got treated like he had some disease. Nobody doubted that the SPCA would stop wagon racing in a minute, if they could.

When the pile-up happened Raymond sprinted out onto the track even before we'd all gotten up. He had the vet with him, and they just did it all on the spot. Euthanized them, as the vet called it, by injection. There were dead horses all over Turn One and most of the people in the stands went off to the beer tent so they wouldn't have to look at it and defend why they were watching something so ugly and so heartbreaking.

Dalton stood in front of me nodding uncertainly. He hooked his thumbs in his belt. "Bugger Raymond'd probably like to hear about it." He squinted at something in the dirt. "But he can do his own work."

I shrugged. Dalton turned without saying anything more, and I was left looking at his retreating back. He was a little bow-legged, and his old jeans were tight just below his big gut but limp and baggy down around his rear end. I pulled my own jeans up a little and went to turn the hose off.

The day after the accident and us finding the weight, I went over to the fairgrounds. It was a hot, kindling-dry day. The rides and everything were situated north of the race track and skirted the road that takes you right out of Ponoka, west on to Highway 53.

It's a fine prairie town, Ponoka, with lots of trees, and abrupt hills rising like a dike over the east edge of the town, but it's also got a reputation, due to the provincial mental hospital there. The hospital's water tower can be seen from the rodeo stands. I'd never known one thing to happen that involved an escaped mental patient—my mom, who worked there as a nurse before marrying my real father, always said they were less violent than so-called normal people—but the name Ponoka was still attached somehow to being mental, which was too bad.

The fairgrounds were crowded for a Thursday afternoon. There was a long lineup for the Skydiver, the only ride at the fair that looked mechanically sound. I stood and watched the Skycars go around and upside down for a while and listened to the people screaming while all their pocket change fell onto the tarmac beneath them.

After a few minutes I turned around and there behind me, staring up, was Raymond. He had on a cowboy hat and wire-rimmed sunglasses, and he wore a neatly trimmed moustache.

"Raymond," I said. "Hi."

He looked at me and rubbed his neck. "Hey, Gordie," he said. "How ya doin?"

"Good," I said. We stood facing one another, and people went around us.

"Lord," he said, looking back at the Skydiver, "put me on that thing and it would rain puke."

"Me too," I said.

"How's your old man?"

"Dalton? Not bad."

"Awful business, eh, that pile-up?"

"Yeah," I said. I looked back at the ride. I liked Raymond. I could sympathize with his job. He probably didn't like having to snoop around, though he was an RCMP constable before he joined the SPCA. The word was that he was squeezed out of the force for beating up some guy who turned out to be innocent. If he'd just shot the guy nothing would have come of it.

"Getting ready for school?"

"You bet," I said. "Just a couple more weeks."

"This is your second year in a row now, isn't it?"

I shrugged. "I'm on a roll, I guess."

"Hey," he said. "That pile-up. How'd that look from your saddle?" He put both his hands in his jeans back pockets and stood with his weight on his heels, which made him lean forward from the waist and seem extra interested.

"Well, Raymond," I said. "There wasn't much I could see. I was just looking ahead, and then suddenly everybody was on everybody else. Except for Leroy. Matter of fact," I continued, "I didn't even hear Alberta's neck snap. Tommy said he heard it."

"Tommy heard that, did he?"

"Says so."

"Course he was a bit further up than you, wasn't he?"

"I was nearer the rail, I guess."

Raymond nodded while he took his hands out of his back pockets. He pulled a hankie out from his shirt pocket and blew his nose. I noticed a pin on his shirt that had the letters SPCA on it. I wondered why he needed to wear that. He'd never worn one before, and everybody knew perfectly well what he did.

"Hmm," he said, after he got his hankie back in his pocket. "Just one of those things, I guess. Billy's lead horse could've got a wasp in his eye or something. Mystery of the universe. Nobody saw nothing. Mister Leroy Dank probably had the cleanest view." Raymond didn't look at me when he said this, so I didn't have to say anything about the weight in Leroy's wagon, or anything else.

"What's this for?" I asked, pointing at the pin.

He sneered and looked down at it. "Orders. They want us to get hats, too."

"Jesus," I said. "That's a joke."

"Yeah," he said. "But not this cowboy." We both laughed.

"I gotta run, Raymond," I lied. "Dalton wants me back to do

some shoeing."

"Better luck tonight," he said, and turned to look at the Sky-diver. I didn't head back to our camp but went instead to the beer tent, betting I'd find Tommy there. If Dalton did by chance want anything done he could always come and find me.

After the race that evening, which Leroy won handily, there was a bit of a get-together just by my mom's and Dalton's trailer, and we got a pretty good fire going. Raymond wandered over and this seemed okay with everyone, mostly because he hadn't been asking too many questions.

It was a warm evening. After a few beers, with the sky so big and clear, I fell silent, which I didn't mind. Sparks from the fire caught the updraft and rode it until they got lost in the stars.

My mom got to telling this story around the fire about my father, her first husband, who died when she was twenty-five and I was not past my first birthday, and how he could never get his truck out of their yard without accidentally running over a chicken or a cat or a gopher or something, swerving two or three differ-ent ways trying to miss it before finally squashing it. She was a comical woman, and the way she told it made you laugh. Dalton sat back with his boots up on a log and chuckled, taking foamy swigs from his beer and scratching himself. He didn't have his hat on, which was unusual, and his dark longish hair fell in strands off the top of his head. This forced him to collect it in the space between his thumb and forefinger and sweep it straight back on to the top of his head, where he would pat it down with the palm of his hand. It would stay that way for about ten seconds before falling forward again like long droopy grass.

Raymond stayed off to the side and laughed uproariously at my mother's story, which surprised me, him being with the SPCA.

Later on, I shuffled half-drunk over to the paddock to have a leak. I didn't feel like going as far as the public washroom, and it was dark anyway. I wasn't long into it when Raymond came up beside me. He unzipped and stood with one hand on his hip and his feet wide apart.

"Hello, Raymond," I said and glanced at him, sidewise.

"Gordie," he said. He was smirking but his eyes were closed.

We finished in silence, and he turned to me and said, "Gordie? See them?"

I looked over and pointed. "The horses?" They were silent, though a couple were nosing at the feed bags hanging from the fence. "Yeah," I said. "I see them."

"Them," he squinted. "Them and you and me." He pointed at them in turn.

"All piss outdoors," I said and laughed.

"Them and you and me," he said more quickly, ignoring me. "We're going to get Leroy." He looked at me straight on and then neither of us were acting like drunks anymore.

"What?"

"Leroy," he said. "For that pile-up."

I looked around and wiped my hands on my backside. "Leroy did that?" I said.

"C'mon, Gordie," he said. "Course he did." He leaned over the fence and put a boot up on the lowest rail.

"Yeah, he probably did, didn't he," I said, putting my hands into my pockets.

"Any ideas?" asked Raymond without looking at me. He continued to lean over the railings and tried to coax one of the horses over to us by snapping his fingers. "About how or why Leroy would do a thing like that?"

"Hadn't really thought about it, I guess."

"No?" He turned and looked at me. His eyes were bright. "Well, I have. He could've loosened a wheel on somebody's rig. Screwed up one of the horses' bits. Sabotaged a rein. Anything. He's a bastard, Gordie. But then they all are, even your old man."

I looked over at him and almost agreed.

He lowered his tone and said, "Sorry."

He looked back to the horses and made some stupid kissing noises. "I asked maybe one question from each of them. Got sweet bugger-all."

I took my hands out of my pockets and didn't know what to do with them, so I put them back. I had to piss again, but that would have been too embarrassing.

"I'm not trying to stop racing, Gordie," he said. "I just hate seeing horses killed."

"Fair enough, Raymond," I said. "But who doesn't? You think Dalton didn't hate losing Alberta?"

"Not as much as he'd hate talking to me about it."

A horse had taken to Raymond snapping his fingers and wandered over. It was Tory, named by Dalton out of his hatred for Pierre Trudeau. Tory was a fine tall chestnut, seven or eight years old. He stood by us and nuzzled Raymond's hand, even though Raymond had nothing in it. I felt sorry for Raymond right then and there. He was a good person and was trying to do something that was not a bad thing—protect animals—but he was dead right; there wasn't going to be anybody helping him out. He seemed like a lot of people to me—stuck in a spot through his or someone else's failings, and also capable of seeing the other spot he wanted to be in but wasn't. And not knowing how to get to that other spot would wear at him like a slow and emptying illness.

"You and me and these guys." He spanked Tory lightly along the neck. "We'll get Leroy."

"I just don't know what you're going on about, with us and the horses. I'm not here to take sides. I like you Raymond, but don't ask me to do things like whatever you have in mind. I'm just here to ride with Dalton for the summer, then I'm going back to school. I'm not interested in anything else."

"Jesus, Gordie. Relax." He shook his head, facing back in the direction of the fire, though it couldn't be seen from where we were. I glanced at him three-quarters on and he looked like a cop right then, with his clipped moustache. His plain stare and lipless grimace were things I'd seen on cops' faces before, at crazy bush parties or bar fights. I was getting cold, and shivered, which made Raymond look over at me. "I'm heading back in a minute." I turned away from him and had a short leak.

"I'll go with you," he said when I'd finished. We started back. Tory snorted at us and walked back to the other side of the pen. We were back at the fire in less than a minute, and it was still burning fiercely, though a lot of people had gone off to bed, my mother and Dalton among them. Tommy was still there, along with a couple of other riders, and they were huddled around one side of the fire. Raymond and I sat down with them, cracked a couple of beers, and started laughing at a story Tommy was telling about some guy's truck and his failed brakes.

The next morning I went back to our ranch, twenty or so miles southwest of Rimbey, to get another horse. It was looking like Dalton might make the semi-finals, and having lost two horses he figured he might need a fresh one if he got to the finals.

Rimbey is an hour's drive west of Ponoka along Highway 53, a two-laner that's as straight as a plank. It crosses under Highway 2, which runs through Alberta like a backbone, and after Highway 2 you've only got to turn once before you hit Rimbey. It was another huge and perfect day and after I crossed under Highway 2 there was no traffic along 53, so I could go as fast as I liked and still look around. The gentle roll of the land reminded me of an unmade bed, flat for the most part with a hill here and there. It was golden, green and fertile, and farmers and ranchers did well in this country.

Just before I got to the nothing hamlet of Crestomere I spotted a couple of hawks hunting gophers on a cropped field. I pulled over and watched for fifteen minutes or so. The gophers must have had holes every few feet because the hawks weren't having much luck. Finally one of the gophers made a mistake and a hawk sank its talons in and was gone, up and over the field to a small bluff of spruce away to the north. I pulled back onto the road and slipped into an easy enjoyment of the straight drive.

Dalton did make the semi-finals, which was an unusually good result for him, and so did Leroy Dank, easily. Raymond had been outwardly ignoring the pile-up and had scarcely said a thing about it since it happened, though I thought he looked at me in a special way every time I saw him—he'd look at me and hardly blink.

Yet Raymond didn't say a word to me. Not that I hadn't been thinking about what he'd said. Tommy, who'd started this whole thing with Leroy's wagon, was the only person I told that Raymond had Leroy under suspicion. Tommy didn't want to say boo to Raymond. "Let him handle it himself," Tommy said, trying to be casual about the whole thing but knowing damn well that if it was Leroy who did it he shouldn't get out of it with his only punishment being more disliked than before.

Saturday, semi-final day, was sun-driven, again hot and dry. The stands, permanent around the outside of the track and temporary in the infield, were full with people down from Edmonton and up from Red Deer for the day. The first semi-final had both Dalton and Leroy in it.

Right out of the barrels Leroy was whipping his team hard with his reins, driving like a madman. Dalton clipped a barrel and came out onto Turn One in last place, already two full lengths behind Leroy and with penalty points for tipping the barrel. I got way ahead of Dalton, practically up beside Leroy, who was whipping his team and bouncing up and down on his seat. He looked obsessed. All drivers sometimes got that way, bug-eyed and hats flying, but Leroy was moving, his horses eating up the dirt in huge gorgeous strides. He was not going to lose. On Turn Two he looked back to see where everybody was, and when he saw me he grinned.

Dalton was still a couple lengths behind me, and at least four behind Leroy. He was viciously slashing at his horses, desperately trying to avoid last place. I rode steady with him when he finally caught up to us outriders. He was glaring at the rig in front of us, like it would matter if he caught it. We did frantically pull even with one of the other teams along the outside of Turn Three, and then Dalton cut him off to try and get a better line to catch the rig in second, which we didn't. I wasn't concentrating so well by this time. It was my last race of the year and I knew we weren't headed for anywhere but home. I accidentally crossed the finish line about half a length ahead of Dalton, which meant more penalty points. It didn't make any difference, but it was still bad riding.

Leroy won it by four lengths in the end. And with all his penalty points Dalton ended up last. This put him in a bad frame of mind. Even though he hadn't expected to win he hated losing to Leroy and seeing him make the final.

After we got the wagon back to camp, I helped Tommy unhitch all the horses and brush the sweat and dirt and straw off of them, which was never a small job. Just twenty yards from where Tommy and I stood was one of the dusty main roads leading out of the campground. There was some traffic on it, that being the day to pack and leave if you hadn't qualified for any of the event finals.

"So Gordo," said Tommy, from the other side of the horse we were brushing. "Another summer gone. You're back to being a scholar now, eh?"

"That's right," I said. "Time to start being brilliant again. Anything you want to know?" I ran my brush hard over the horse's shoulder. It was a big strong animal, and he rocked while we brushed him, snorting occasionally from deep inside his chest.

"You being brilliant," Tommy said. "Shit, I'd like to see that."

I spit at him over the horse's back, missing on purpose.

"You spit like you ride," he said.

Dalton shuffled over from across the camp just as we were finishing the second of four horses. He was sweaty and dirty, and looked like maybe he needed a brushing, too. He stood and watched Tommy and me for a minute before saying anything.

"I want you to hurry up with these horses," he said, to me only. "Then go and help your mother load the wagon."

I wanted to ask him why he wasn't helping her load the wagon. "About an hour," I said.

"If it takes you two an hour to brush two goddamned horses, I'll hire someone else to ride for me next year." He wasn't joking. He stood there and looked at me like I was a dead dog on the road, like something he'd gotten a close look at but didn't want to touch. "I may get me some new outriders next year, anyway. Some that can help me win." His lips went tight and thin. Then he turned around and walked off. I wanted to shout after him and tell him I was glad he didn't make the final, but I held my tongue.

It took us about forty-five minutes to do the horses and then another hour or so to get the wagon all loaded and on the trailer. After that my mom and Dalton left, carrying the horse-trailer behind them. Tommy was to drive the wagon-trailer back, but we decided to hit the beer tent for our last rodeo beer of the summer. The tent was crowded with people who had the same idea as us, and it took about ten minutes just to get to the beer counter. We stood outside and caught some sun as we drank. Two weren't enough, so Tommy went to get four more and I held our spot. While Tommy was gone Raymond walked by, on the outside of the yellow rope fence that marked the beer tent boundary. He didn't see me at first.

"Raymond," I said loudly. "Hey there."

"Gordie." He came over. "How ya doin?"

"Good, good," I said. "Done for another year and that feels all right."

"I bet." He paused and then said, "I never did find anything on Leroy. For that pile-up."

"No?"

"It was him, though. Trust me."

"Well, you know, Raymond, nobody likes the guy anyway."

Raymond's face closed like a book. "That doesn't mean fuck-all to me. He killed horses."

We stood quiet for a few seconds.

"Just in case you wondered," Raymond said, back in level voice, "I didn't ask anybody else for help."

"I didn't wonder." I looked to see if Tommy was coming.

Raymond nodded slowly and pushed out his lower lip. "Well," he said, "Leroy won't get away with any more of that shit from now on. I'm on him."

"Good."

Raymond looked at his watch. "I gotta get going, Gordie. Have one for me." He made a drinking motion with his hand.

"I will," I said. "Couple maybe."

"Good. And good luck in school."

"Thanks." We shook hands above the yellow rope, grazing it, and then he left.


I spent the next ten days riding and walking around the ranch, especially out where Habit Creek cuts through the corner of our westernmost quarter section. This was well west of Rimbey, where the land really started to predict mountains and it was mostly into pure tree country. The foothills were under your feet when you stood out there, and if you found yourself at the top of a hill and turned all the way around once and looked at the landscapes within your sight, you would swear there wasn't anything more beautiful on this earth, with the sun banking white rays off the Rocky Mountains sixty miles to the southwest, and the hugeness of the prairies, like a dry rolling ocean bed, extending eastward all the way to Lake Winnipeg and beyond, though you knew you could only see thirty or forty miles at best.

After those ten days I kissed my mother on the cheek, grabbed hands briefly with Dalton, and went back to Edmonton for my second year of university. I would see them again at Christmas, and I would talk with my mother on the phone once every two weeks, when she would ask me about my school work and my money situation. I hadn't given much thought at all to the rodeo during those ten days but I did when I was driving north to Edmonton. I thought mostly of Raymond, because I figured he was a decent man, and I still do think that. I saw him on the circuit the next two summers running and never once did he talk to me about Leroy. On the third year following, the SPCA transferred him and his wife and kid to Peace River. I didn't see him again after that, which was no bitter tragedy because we never got closer than we did the summer of the pile-up, which wasn't all that close.

I didn't know what these events meant to me at the time and only now can I say that I might have done something to help Raymond, even if it had only been to show him some support. Who knows if anything would've changed as a result anyway, though I know that's not the point. I hadn't helped him, but I don't blame myself for that. Tommy could have helped him just as easily.

But I think I understand now that opportunities like the one Raymond presented to me will pass through a person's life at different and unpredictable times. I think that's true. When another chance shows itself to me, I'll see it for what it is and act on it, if it's the right thing to do.

▲▲▲▲▲▲

# THE MEAT LOCKER

▲▲▲▲▲▲

**K**eith, the chef, had me in a headlock. "You pimply little shit!" he said. The steak knife I'd accidentally speared him with was in his hand and he held it to my neck. "If I wasn't on parole, I'd slit your fucking throat!"

His face was close enough to my own that I could have gotten my teeth on his beard. I could smell liquor on his breath. He was talking fast, his voice a saw, sharp and raspy. He normally yelled a lot on the job, at me and everyone else, but this was different. I was scared this time.

The other busboys and myself had been hanging out in the kitchen, taking turns throwing knives into a wooden wall. We were aiming at a tiny metal bolt and one of my tosses hit it, bounced straight left over a salad cart, and hit Keith in the fore-arm, really only nicking him.

"Keith, come on, man," said my friend Doug, another busboy. "It was an accident. He wasn't aiming for you or anything." A couple of the other busboys left for their sections despite the fact that Bluebeard's was practically empty.

Will, the maitre d', came gliding into the kitchen, cool as ever, each hair in place.

"Keith," he said slowly, "put that knife down and let Norman go."

Keith took the knife away from my throat but kept me in the headlock. "Suck my dick, you fairy!" he said to Will.

I couldn't really see Keith's face, but it wasn't hard to imagine crazy eyes. And I was certain his eyes looked different than they had earlier in the evening, when I'd arrived before Bluebeard's opened. As I came in the delivery door Keith was having an argument with a woman. Will was there, shifting around uncomfortably, as if he'd happened upon the scene, too. The woman was saying nasty things to Keith, personal things. She didn't like his anger. She didn't like the way he treated her like a goddess one day and a whore the next. That she'd had it. It seemed final. She'd left in a flurry, brushing past me.

Will and I had stood there like onlookers at a crash. Keith silently retreated to the kitchen without making eye contact. I felt sorry for him, and would have said something if I'd had any idea what would make him feel better. We'd had the occasional conversation, and he was a friendly guy when he was calm, though he was not the most popular person at the restaurant. But this knife thing had set him off. It was as if he suddenly didn't know me.

A tight circle had formed around Keith and me. My face was right up against his hairy forearm. Out of one eye I could see a lot of people from the waist down. With the other eye I could see livid purple marks, like worms, up and down Keith's arm. Kos, the sous chef, had said they were razor blade scars.

Will took a step inward. "Keith," he said calmly. "There are customers. And may I remind you that Oscar and Klara gave you this job on the provision you remained amiable. This is not amiable. Your job is at risk."

My neck was aching and Keith jerked it a couple of times like he was preparing for a wrestling move. Then he let go. I didn't move except to straighten up. He took a fistful of my hair and put the knife in my face again.

"Don't you ever, ever, fuck with me like that again. Understand?"

I didn't say anything, just kept staring straight ahead, at everybody else. Then he let go of my hair and went back to his grill. He pulled a slip off the order wheel and went on with his work as if nothing had taken place.

I had a bad kink in my neck and spots in my vision. My scalp hurt. I was mad at Keith at that moment, because I'd never done anything to him. The knife was an accident. No wonder people talked about him. He was there only because Klara's dead husband Oscar felt sorry for him. Oscar also had had some war thing with Keith's dad. Cooking was not a problem for Keith, but he could be a maniac.

"Thank you, Keith," said Will, who then motioned at me to come with him into the back. I followed him around behind the kitchen.

"Now, Norman," he said. "I think Keith has acted horribly. I can't imagine you did anything to deserve this." He paused. "Did you?"

"I stuck him in the arm with a knife."

Will closed his eyes and took a breath.

"Why don't you have a piece of cheesecake. Then you can take the rest of the night off."

"I'm okay," I said. "I'll finish."

He made a face that said, Suit yourself. "Please don't tell your mother about this. Or Klara." He looked in the direction of Klara's office, where she sat brooding over Oscar's recent death almost every evening, emerging only when the place thinned out.

Will headed back to the front of the house. I didn't much like Will, and after he was out of sight I turned and went straight to Klara's office. The door was open, so I looked in. She was lying on a couch. Her hands were in her lap and she was moaning softly.

"Are you okay?" I said.

She shifted to a sitting position. Mascara dust ringed her eyes. It was impossible to tell how old she was. Most of us busboys lusted after her because she was attractive in a distracted, kinky sort of way. Guesses on her age varied between twenty-five and forty, though I personally figured it was closer to forty. She wore black all the time, out of mourning for Oscar, she said, but it was generally clothing that involved a lot of Spandex and tight t-shirts.

From her office couch she looked at me without a hint of recognition. "Who are you?"

"Norman," I replied. "One of the busboys." I asked her again if she was okay.

She regarded me for a moment. "I am not feeling okay," she finally said. "I'm feeling positively murderous."

"So is Keith."

"Keith?"

"Will wanted me to come and tell you that Keith threatened to kill one of the busboys. Put a knife to his throat. It was me, actually."

Klara put a thin hand to her bright red lips. "Keith, Keith." She ran a hand through her hair and said almost to herself, "That man is running out of grace." Then she looked at me to indicate I could leave if I didn't have any more information.

I took a step back.

"Norman," she said. The mascara made her look like a weird sexy raccoon. "Thank you."

Going back through the kitchen, I avoided the grill and went straight to my section.

The next day I came in a couple hours early with Doug, my friend who'd tried to reason with Keith. Kos, the old Greek sous chef, was sitting in a corner of the restaurant, cutting up some fresh herbs. He didn't often work in the kitchen before opening because he and Keith did not get along.

Kos motioned for us to come over to him. The whole corner smelled sharply of basil, though his body odour fought through it. A big dark eyebrow crossed Kos's forehead unbroken and he had a matching bushy moustache that gleamed navy blue in certain lights. He looked like Stalin.

"Norman, I hear," he said gravely. "If only Oscar were still here. He would not be scared to fire such an animal. He's pig, Keith. He should be slaughtered like pig. Hung upside down and stuck in the throat with long-bladed knife then left to bleed into a hole in the ground like pig!" He hacked at some basil.

"I'll leave the knives to him," I said. "I almost didn't live to finish university."

"We must get revenge." He pointed theatrically to Doug, who flinched. "Eh, Doug!" He said it like "dog."

"We will think of something," he continued. "I know about revenge." Kos had been a teenaged soldier in the Greek Civil War in the late forties. We all heard the stories, usually after closing. Keith could always get Kos's goat by saying Kos had only been a cook in the war. Whereas Keith's father had been to Korea with the Princess Patricia Light Infantry, had been badly wounded, and received the Victoria Cross. So the stories went.

"Whatever you say, Kos." I punched Doug on the arm. "Eh, Dog!"

Doug giggled nervously. Kos stared back at us, then broke into a wide grin. He had big cheeks, and when he smiled it looked like he was hiding golf balls in them.

Doug and I went through the restaurant into the back. The staff room was in the basement, and we were headed there to goof off for half an hour before having to come up and fold napkins in that fan pattern that nobody ever pays attention to. Klara insisted on it, claiming it added class.

We had to pass through the kitchen and Keith was there, slicing beef tenderloin into filets, meticulously carving away fat but leaving enough to give it some flavour. He looked up as we came into the kitchen and stopped what he was doing. Doug disappeared down the stairs without looking back, but I hung back.

"Hey, Keith," I said, my voice wavering. I stood with my arms at my side.

Keith took a small step towards me. I didn't have any sense of what he was going to do. His expression was calm, kind of serious. He still had the filet knife in one hand, but he held both hands out as though in apology. Kos walked into the section of the kitchen Keith and I were in. He was carrying his metal bowl full of freshly cut basil.

"Ho!" he said, stepping in between the two of us.

"No, no," I said. "Relax, Kos." I could smell the basil and Kos.

Keith looked at Kos. "Just leave," Keith said.

"Is everything all right, Norman," said Kos. "Really?"

I nodded. Kos looked back at Keith, who was smiling. "I don't know why Klara does not fire you," he said to Keith. "Oscar would have done."

Once Kos had left, Keith tried to apologize to me.

"Last night," he said. "I mean..." He shook his head and stared down at the floor, not out of shame, but just in the struggle for words.

"Don't sweat it," I said.

"No," he said, looking up. "No excuse." He turned back to the cutting board, so I started for the basement. Before I got out of the kitchen I heard Keith give a little yelp. I ran back to the table he was standing at. He was holding his left hand with his right. The tip of his left thumb was gone, and he was bleeding all over the place.

"Keith!" I said. "Oh, gross!"

He immediately put the knife down and rushed into the back for the first aid kit, holding his hand in his apron, which was rapidly turning scarlet. The tip of this thumb sat like a button on the cutting board. I didn't think I could just leave it there, the thumb piece, so I picked it up and wrapped it in a napkin. I went into the fridge, and put it on the same shelf as the eggs, cream, milk and cheese. When I came out Will had taken Keith to the hospital for stitches.

About an hour later, just before opening, Klara came into the restaurant saying she needed someone to help her with an errand. All the busboys and waiters were preparing for the shift, or just doing nothing. It was a fun time to be around the restaurant. I'd held the floor for a good thirty minutes with the story of Keith's thumb. The gossip stopped when Klara walked in.

"I need someone," she said. "To come with me to get some packages."

One of the waiters got up. "I'll give you a hand," he said.

"No," said Klara. "I pay you too much to have you lift boxes." She pointed at me. "You. What's your name?"

"Norman. I saw you last night. I'm the one Keith tried to kill."

She stared at me through her racoon eyes. "Yes, of course." The words were hardly out of her mouth before she had turned around for the back door. I followed her.

Klara's car was spectacularly vulgar. It was a powder blue Lincoln Continental, an older one, two doors, about forty feet long, and it had deep plush burgundy seat covering. There was a fuzzy sheepskin thing covering the steering wheel. The engine roared like a bus when she turned the key, and she must have thought that all men are by birth obsessed with engines, because she attempted to make conversation by telling me about this one.

"Four hundred and fifty four cubic inches," she said. "Eight cylinders. Two hundred and forty horses."

I had my arms folded over my chest. "Oh, yeah."

She glanced at me as we pulled out of the parking lot. "You don't like cars?"

"Sure," I said. "I like cars."

The sun was still shining and she brought down her sun visor, eyeing me skeptically once she had the brightness out of her eyes. "How about girls? Women?"

"Yes!" I said, trying to sound indignant. "Why?"

"Oh, nothing, nothing," she said. "Will hires very good staff but a lot of fags, that's all." Her hands were coming off the steering wheel as she drove, frequently both at the same time. I found this disconcerting. She had rings on every finger except her ring finger, and she was constantly adjusting and twisting them.

"Listen, Norman," she said. "I know who you are."

My head craned forward a little. "You do?"

"Yes. I was only pretending to not remember who you were in front of the other staff."

I nodded, unsure of where she was headed, conversationally or otherwise. She seemed to be paying no attention whatsoever to our direction, and turned here and there without really looking.

"There's something we need to talk about," she continued. "I need to talk about. You can do something for me. It's about Keith. I need you to talk to him. He likes you. He doesn't like anybody else."

"He doesn't like me at all!" I cried. "He nearly killed me last night."

She took both hands off the wheel and made waving motions. "No, no," she said. "Keith was upset about something else. Will told me it was a woman. It wasn't you."

"Well, what makes you think he likes me?" I asked, my voice still high. "We don't exactly hang out."

A taxi cut her off, and it was just good fortune she had her hands on the wheel. She swerved and honked.

"You asshole!" she shouted. "People," she said, in exasperation, "cannot drive. It's a fact."

Once she had her composure back she ignored my question.

"Keith is a difficult person for me to talk to," she said. "It was always Oscar that talked to him. I need you to tell him I'm closing the restaurant."

"Closing the restaurant!? What about the rest of us?"

"I'm sorry," she said. "But I'm losing all kinds of money. Poor Oscar would kill me, but I have to eat, too. This restaurant is a loser. Nobody's eating steak and lobster anymore. They're eating goat cheese pizzas and pasta primavera. Anyway, I just can't tell Keith. I don't have the guts. You don't even have to tell him. Just drop hints about how bad business is. Then maybe say you're sure the place is going under. You know, stuff like that. I just don't think he'd take it very well to be told straight out, especially by me. I want to prepare him. I don't have the heart to tell him. It'll devastate him. His father and Oscar were such good friends."

"But what about everybody else? When are you going to tell them?"

She fiddled with her rings and adjusted the car stereo. "I'll give them at least two weeks notice." She put her hands back on the wheel and gave me a sidelong glance. "Except you, of course. I'm sure I'll find something for you."

The evening went quickly, as it was a surprisingly busy night. I wanted Klara down on the floor to show her there were still people interested in steak and lobster, but I didn't go near her office. I had to admit to myself I was flattered by Klara singling me out to speak to Keith, even if it was only because she was a coward. It made me feel like I was the kind of person you could count on in tough spots. I had that reputation as a busboy, too. The maitre d' always assigned me the busiest sections.

Chances to say something to Keith were few that evening

because it was so busy, but after it quieted down, around ten, he went and stood by the back door to have a smoke. I made a pretence of taking some garbage out. After I'd dumped it, I stopped by him on the way back in.

"Slow night, eh?"

He took his cigarette out of his mouth. "Where the fuck were you all night?"

"Tonight wasn't so bad. But it's been brutal lately."

"Yeah," he said. "Wouldn't surprise me if she shuts the place down."

I gaped at him. "What!?"

"She hates this place," he said. "Oscar ran it, not her."

"Do you think she'd do it?" I asked. "I mean, shut the place down?"

"Maybe," he said. "Not my problem, anymore."

"What do you mean?"

He had one last drag and then flicked the butt out into the alley. "Just not my problem anymore, that's all."

"But you won't have a job if she closes the restaurant."

There was no response from him, but I didn't feel at all like that meant he wanted me to leave.

"So what does Kos have against you?"

Keith shrugged. "He thinks I'm bad for the restaurant. And Klara." He lit up another cigarette and took a deep first drag. "He figures he's got to protect her now that Oscar's gone."

We stood silently for a minute. "How's your thumb?"

The bandage was faintly red at the tip and he held it up to inspect it. "It hurts."

I nodded. "Sorry. I probably distracted you."

He kept examining his thumb, looking at it from all angles, pinching it and flexing it. "I deserved it. Anyways, got to feel something, sometimes."

It occurred to me that he was making a vague reference to his ex-girlfriend and the argument I'd seen earlier. But my desire at that point was to not insult him, so I didn't ask him what he meant. I had no idea.

"You know, Klara asked me to mention stuff to you about the restaurant closing. Like dropping hints and stuff. She said she didn't want to talk to you about it."

A hand went to his beard and he started gently pulling on it. After a minute or two of this, he started crying. With no warning or even any sounds, a few tears trickled down his cheeks and disappeared into the brush of his beard. He folded his arms over his chest. I stood there for at least another five minutes but he didn't say a word. After a couple of minutes I lost that feeling of him not wanting me to leave. I said something to him about getting back inside and left him there.

The restaurant was empty of customers now and some of the staff were sitting around the tables, cashing out and counting tips. I went to use the staff washroom, and down the hallway I could see light shining out from under Klara's door. I thought I might tell her I had at least talked with Keith.

I put my hand on the office doorknob. It was locked and didn't rotate, but the door itself was slightly ajar. I couldn't hear anything so I just pushed it open and put my head and shoulder through. Klara was lying on the couch in the same way she had been the night before when I went to her office. This time she had her hand down the front of her black pants. I could see fingershapes undulating under the surface of the spandex. I must have made some sound, because she whipped around and looked at me.

"Shut that goddamn door," she hissed. I stepped inside and shut it behind me. She still had her hand in her pants.

"Didn't your mother teach you to knock," she said. "Jesus Christ." She sat up on the couch and removed her hand.

"Sorry," I said, hoarsely. "Sorry."

"That's okay." She pushed her tongue against the inside of her cheek, and then said, "I was just thinking about you, anyway."

She got off the couch and went over to a cabinet, where she poured herself a drink. It was pastel coloured, and looked sweet and syrupy. She made me one, and when she handed it to me I could smell her on the glass. She sat back down on the couch and crossed her legs.

"So aren't I embarrassed," she said.

I took a sip of my drink.

She patted the couch beside her. I went and sat down, though at the far end. She moved a little closer to me.

"Are there any people left out there?"

"Some staff."

She nodded. "Now tell me, did you have a chance yet to talk to Keith?

I nodded. "Just a little while ago," I said, wondering what I was going to say next.

"Good for you," she said, clinking her glass against mine. "And?"

"He didn't say much."

"Surprise, surprise. Did he say anything about me?"

I had another swig of my drink. It was sweet and tasted a lot like coconut. "Not really," I said.

She seemed disappointed. "Is that right." She put her drink on the table beside the couch, and wiggled a bit closer to me again, so that our thighs were touching.

"Do you have a woman, Norman?"

I smiled and finished off my drink. "Just my mom."

Klara let out a low and slow laugh, like she was laughing to kill time while she thought of something to say or do. She looked intently at me, and then she placed her hand over mine on my thigh.

"You know exactly what you're doing, don't you, Norman?" she said, staring right into me. "I know you do."

Without waiting for me to answer she raised my hand to her

breast, and took her own hand away, placing it along my bicep. I left my hand where it was and squeezed. After I did that, she tightened her grip on my upper arm and pulled me towards her. She leaned back and adjusted herself along the couch. I followed and stretched out on top of her, working at the spandex.

It couldn't have been fifteen minutes later that I left the office. I almost felt like I had to leave right then and there, like the time allotted to me was up. Doing it again with Klara, though, was something I would not turn down. She stood right behind me just before I opened the door, and reached around front to fondle me.

When I opened the door, and stepped into the hallway, I saw Keith at the end of it. He was leaning against the wall.

"Keith!" I said. "Hey."

He was looking past me.

"Shit," said Klara. "Shit." She closed the door behind me and locked it. Keith looked at me briefly and walked back into the kitchen, leaving me alone in the long narrow space of the hallway.

It was my responsibility to open the next day, which meant coming in about an hour earlier than everybody else to vacuum and do the bathrooms. Only the busboys were on the rotation. Generally the cooks, and sometimes Klara, were the only other people in the restaurant at that time.

Kos was in his corner, not yet cutting herbs but just leafing through a sauce book. He didn't acknowledge me as I came in. I asked him where Keith was and he grunted that he hadn't seen him since the night before.

Keith wasn't at the grill or the cutting board. I checked the bathroom. No one was there, or in the staff room. I wanted to say something to Keith, even just hello. The restaurant itself was empty, except for Kos.

Back in the kitchen, I sat on a chair and wondered what I

should start with, the vacuuming or the bathrooms. My decision was to start with a piece of pecan pie. Then I saw a chef's hat, Keith's, sitting on the counter in the corner right by the meat locker, and on the floor was a clean apron.

My legs went rubbery as I stood up and went over to the corner. The hat and apron were spotless. Suddenly, I didn't want to open that locker, but I did. The cold air hit me and froze the sweat on my face. Through the mist the first thing I saw were Keith's feet, about a foot off the floor. I went in and closed the door behind me. He was hanging by an extension cord rigged to the lighting fixture. There was a complete stillness inside. A slight hum emanated from the fluorescent bulbs, and there was a distant rattle from the refrigeration unit. I didn't really need to look because nothing flowed from him, not energy, not life. Not anger or pain, love or hate. Just coldness, much like everything else in that frigid room. I touched his leg and he swayed slightly. I did finally look and I ended up staring for longer than I should have. His face had no expression, he might have been asleep. The tip of his left thumb still had a bandage around it, and his arms dangled crookedly away from his body, as if he were poised to draw.

As I came out of the meat locker, Klara was just coming into the kitchen. I closed the door behind me, and knew I would never go in there again.

"Have you seen Keith?" she asked.

I picked up Keith's apron and hat, and fidgeted with them. "No," I said, then I said, "Yes." Tears were gathering in my eyes but I didn't want to cry, not in front of Klara. I handed her the apron and hat.

"I quit," I said, half-choking on the words. Klara looked at me with her racoon eyes, baffled, as I passed her. She said nothing, but looked at the door of the meat locker. I went down to the staff room. Changing out of my staff shirt, and putting on my own, I popped a button from near the collar, and watched it roll under the lockers. I didn't concern myself with retrieving it and blindly stuffed the rest of my things into a track bag. When I had it all together I went upstairs and, avoiding the kitchen, got out through the delivery door.

▲▲▲▲▲▲▲

# THERE'S A RUSSIAN TANKER
# STUCK IN THE HARBOUR

My greatest fear about going to university in Scotland was that Helen would be right. I cared enough for her that I didn't want to hurt her or have her think badly of me, but when she hugged me goodbye at the airport I held her only briefly and let go before she did. She loved me, she said. She also said I was running away from our relationship because it wasn't perfect, that I might end up being someone who would always run away.

My first day in St Andrews was spent sleeping off the jet lag. The second day I walked around the town. There are two main streets in St Andrews, South Street and North Street, the latter of which trails down to the North Sea and the famous Old Course. It was a balmy early October day and I walked around the Old Course for an hour or so. The Mecca of golf, as it is known, looked more like a neglected farmer's field than the spiritual bosom of the game. The Old Course, and the four other courses in St Andrews, sat on a huge spit of land poking out into the North Sea, and looking across it I couldn't see one tree. There was a lot of thorny scrub and brown grass. I was greatly disappointed at first, since I'd chosen the University of St Andrews largely for the golf. It wasn't until many rounds later that I came to appreciate the subtlety of the Old Course. There was an awesome natural design at work, a course that had not so much been built as allowed to evolve. It was in perfect harmony with the shallow swales and dunes it sat on, and that spit of land could not have had anything on it but the Old Course.

After walking around the course I tried to go inside the Royal and Ancient Golf Club of St Andrews, which is located right between the eighteenth green of the Old Course and the sea wall. There was a military-looking man with a small moustache in the lobby. He volunteered the information that Sean Connery and Dennis Thatcher were members, but wouldn't let me past the reception desk when I made a move to go inside.

"Members only," he said haughtily. "No tourists."

"I'm not a tourist," I said. I loitered for five or ten minutes to annoy him, but he stared at me impassively and bared his teeth in a forced smile when I left.

After leaving the Royal and Ancient I walked back up North Street into town and came across the Whey Pat Tavern. I went inside and it was there that I first saw Gareth, whom I did not actually meet until the next day. Gareth became a good friend in St Andrews, though I haven't seen or heard from him in six years now.

When I ordered a pint the bartender gave me a glass of dark warm liquid. The pub was quite full, but there was some room over at the end of a long table in the corner, so I took my pint over there and sat down. There was a bunch of young guys at the other end of the table. They were laughing and swearing a lot about something. One of them, Gareth, got up on the table and loudly announced: "I am going for a pish!" His glasses were too big for his head and he had buck teeth. "And get me another jar while I'm gone, for Chrissakes!" After making his announcement he got down and went off to the washroom.

The stuff the bartender had given me was bitter and disgusting, and I left it almost untouched. After leaving the Whey Pat I went back to the Post-Graduate Students Residence, a modern, cheaply-constructed dorm located inland. On my way there I wandered through the streets and beautiful buildings of the old town, along the sea wall, and then back up along the waterfront, stopping briefly, awestruck, in front of the centuries-old ruins of the town's first church. The steeple was the only part still standing, and it shot into the sky like a stone spear.

It was October, and though St Andrews was far enough north that the sunlight slanted at a severe angle, the air was crisp and warm, which was not what I expected from a seaside town. Crisp and warm air did not penetrate my room, however, nor did it seem to penetrate anywhere indoors in the whole of the country. The space heater I'd been provided in the absence of central heating did little to improve matters. I sat in my one chair and flipped through some books I'd brought with me. The pages felt sticky. I made my bed, brushed my teeth, and then, with no options left, figured I might as well go to the library to see if I could come up with a good academic reason for being in Scotland.

The next day was blustery but still warm, and little troops of cloud scuttled low across the sky. There were about forty male students milling around the first tee of the Old Course. A guy wearing a University of St Andrew's Golf Team hat was standing near the starter's booth with a clipboard.

"Can I put my name down?" I asked him.

"Sure," he said. "Are you a Yank?"

I shook my head. "Fraser," I said. "Sean Fraser."

"Sean Fraser," he said slowly, as he wrote it down. "You'll be waiting a while here, but we'll get you out."

I stood around watching people tee off. From behind the first tee and eighteenth green, which were side by side, you could see a good part of the town, the Royal and Ancient, the undergraduate residence, Hamilton Hall, and the waves of the North Sea breaking along the beach just beyond the course.

After about thirty minutes my name was called and I was put in a foursome with Gareth and two others. We teed off, and walking down the first fairway I said to Gareth, "I saw you yesterday at the Whey Pat Tavern."

"Fuck me sideways," he said, rolling his eyes heavenward. "I was pished out of my skull."

"That was pretty obvious."

"Dear oh dear," he said, shaking his head in mock embarrassment. "My overdraft is a disaster. Two pounds turns into ten just like that. My dad's going to sack me if he's got any sense."

He shot 75 and I shot 74. We played together the next day, both shot 74, made the University Golf Team, and attended an introductory dinner that evening for the ten members of the team, plus coaches. The beer flowed as if from an inexhaustible source. I stumbled home at two a.m.

The next morning I got up at seven to meet Knellman, my advisor, for the first time. When I got to his office door, I stopped and listened because I could hear muttering on the other side. The words were indistinguishable, but he seemed to be lecturing. Then I thought he might be berating the student so I waited to hear another voice, but no other sounds came through. After a few minutes of hearing only his droning voice, I knocked. The sound ended instantly, and the door shot open, revealing a hunted-looking short man with stiff hair and shallow eye-sockets.

"Fraser!" he exclaimed. "This must be he."

After leading me into his fantastically overcrowded office, and moving a pile of papers off a chair for me, he got down to business.

"Now then, Fraser," he said, leaning his elbows on his desk. "Do you play the grand old game?"

I told him I'd made the team and he was suitably impressed.

"We must get a game, then, young man. Imperative." He pulled on a rogue eyebrow that was at least two inches long. "And kill a couple of pints afterwards at my club, I should think."

"Absolutely," I said. "Whenever you like."

He looked at his watch. "I shouldn't think they're very busy at the moment," he said. "I believe we could make good use of our time together on the course to discuss your topic, of which I am currently in the proverbial dark. Shall I ring over to the course, then?"

The phone was in his hand, and he paused, looked over, waited for me to say yes or no. It was clearly a moment with disastrous potential, one that he was going to be able to hold against me either way if things went badly in the end. This was going to be evidence that from the start I was, depending on my choice here, either too serious or gravely without focus.

I shrugged and smiled. "Why not."

The Post-Graduate Students Residence was a damp, cold and dismal place. In a town teeming with stunning old stone buildings it stood out as completely characterless, and so I moved out before the first week was up. I had been walking around the town and saw a sign in a window along a street of elegant granite houses that said, "Room for Rent." When I rang the bell a tall and attractive but slightly heavy young woman answered. She smiled brightly.

"Hi," I said. "I see you've got a room for rent."

"Yes!" she said. "Yes, come in."

Like every other building in St Andrews it was colder inside than outside, so I kept my jacket on.

"I'm Sheilagh," she said, smiling openly.

"Sean." I held out my hand. She took it and grasped it so hard that I instantly responded with extra pressure of my own in case she thought I was some kind of weakling. She pumped my hand vigorously and then wiped her palm on her trousers when she finished.

There were four students living in the house, and they wanted a fifth to cut costs. Sheilagh led me to a door on the second floor of the three-floor walkup. She snapped her fingers lightly as we climbed.

"I imagine it's a little small by your North American standards," she said, opening the room door. "But it's quite cozy, actually."

"It's a closet!" I said, teasing her. "That room's not big enough to change my mind in!"

Sheilagh let out a delightful laugh at my old joke. She turned her head and looked at me askew while she laughed.

"Do you think I could even fit a bed in there?" I asked, laughing with her.

"Don't be a wet blanket!" she said. "A single, of course. We have one in the attic."

"Maybe I'll take the attic," I said. "It must be bigger."

Over a cup of tea I discovered she was an economics major and was on the ladies golf team.

"And what are you studying?" she asked.

"I'm doing my doctorate," I said. I liked the word doctorate. "In British history."

"What area?"

"Not sure, to be honest. I've met with my advisor twice, and we haven't talked about me yet, though I do know his family history, the outline of his seminal first book, how many pints he can drink in a sitting, and the fact that he is a horrible golfer."

Sheilagh laughed again and seemed content just listening to whatever I had to say. She was friendly and polite, but artless. Her little gestures, the palm-wiping and finger-snapping, made her seem completely without guile or self-consciousness. Even as I thought it I didn't like the trite way it sounded, but I couldn't help thinking that she seemed very genuine. I stayed the rest of the afternoon, and she invited me to stay for dinner.

Afterwards, Sheilagh drove me back to the Residence and

helped me pick up my things. As it turned out, a single bed did just fit in my new room, but the house was still more comfortable than the cheerless dorm I'd left. I met and chatted with the rest of my new roommates and it was close to midnight by the time Sheilagh and I had the room all set up. I had to drop a few good-natured hints about my tiredness before she finally went up to her own room.

One evening, about six weeks after I moved in, Sheilagh and I made plans to go for dinner. She wanted to take me to the Peat Inn, a quaint little restaurant up on a large hill behind town. The spectacular view took in the Eden River estuary leading out to the North Sea, and at night you could see the lights of Dundee twenty kilometres up the coast.

Before dinner, though, I had arranged to meet Gareth at the Jigger Pub down by the Road Hole, the seventeenth hole, of the Old Course. This was a pub we knew well, having spent nearly as much time there as we did playing golf three or four times a week. Gareth insisted I meet him that afternoon. When I got there I had a hard time finding him because the pub was packed, mostly with cliques of gnarled old caddies hunched over their pints with butts hanging out of their toothless mouths. I found Gareth in a corner sitting by himself.

"Sean, you pishtank!" he said. He'd had a few already by the looks of it, and he leered a bit as he spoke.

"Hey, Gareth," I said. I slipped in behind the table more or less beside him, so that we could look out over the pub. He had two full pints in front of him and pushed one in front of me.

"Get that down your neck," he said, concentrating on not spilling any while he moved it. His eyes looked huge behind his thick glasses.

I took a sip and smacked my lips. "So what's the news?"

He looked in his pint and then back up to me. His eyes were liquid and watery.

"I've been sacked."

"What?! What do you mean?"

"I'm out. My dad pulled my stipend. The bastard. I'm a bit over at the bank, but he's gone and told them not to give me any more money."

I paused. "So what does that mean? You have nothing?"

"Tuition is paid. And my hall fees. Other than that I've got shite."

"You're not going to have to quit are you?" I would have been quite upset if he'd left, as Gareth was really the only male friend I'd made in St Andrews.

"No, no," he said. "He's just trying to force me to pick my marks up, the punter. I'll just be a bit dry for a few weeks." He rubbed his thumb and forefinger together. "Until my mom brings him around, that is."

"Don't worry," I said. "I'll cover you."

He picked up his pint and clinked it against mine. "Cheers."

Most of the rest of the afternoon was spent offering him a sort of consolation, although his major concern was that he wasn't going to have enough money to buy beer. Luckily, he was on the Golf Team, so he didn't have to pay to play.

"What about that skirt you're living with?" he asked, after we'd consumed a few more. "She's well off. Looks it, anyway."

"I don't know," I said. "I suppose she is. She doesn't seem to have a problem buying whatever she wants to buy, which really isn't all that much."

"You want her?"

"Meaning?"

"She's got the dewy for you, my friend."

I shrugged. "She's nice," I said. "She's a wonderful person."

"A bit fat."

"You're a real beer swilling pillock, Gareth, you know that." I gave him a swipe and his glasses came off one ear. I looked at my watch. "Anyway, I've got to go. Dinner at the Peat Inn."

He fixed his glasses and let out a groan. "The Peat Inn! Thank you very fucking much. That's a bit posh."

"I'm not paying."

"Well, don't forget about tomorrow. Ten o'clock, old man. The Old Course."

"See you on the tee." I left him alone at the table and as I was leaving I looked back to wave. He wasn't following me out but was staring intently into his pint, as if he was trying to gauge exactly how much was left and how he ought to go about drinking it.

The Peat Inn was not crowded when Sheilagh and I got there, but by eight o'clock every table was full. We'd arrived at six because Sheilagh had wanted to make sure we got a table by the big old fireplace, into which a waiter tossed a large hairy chunk of peat moss every hour or so.

"This is brilliant," she said. "It's so warm here. Whenever I'm feeling cold I like to come here, even if it's just to have a drink at nights."

"It is a great place," I said. Beams hung low over the tables and in certain sections there was just enough headroom to stand up. People spoke in low tones. Farm implements hung on the walls, but it was clearly an expensive restaurant. We ordered fish caught that morning in the North Sea and purchased from the dock market at Crail, just down the coast from St Andrews.

"So tell me about life back home," Sheilagh said, after we'd had our meals.

"Life back home?" I pushed out my lips a little. "Life back home was fine."

Sheilagh folded her napkin and leaned forward. "But you decided to come here." She smiled and primly folded her hands on the table in front of her. "I'm not complaining, of course."

I smiled back. "I just needed a change."

"From?"

"Oh, you know. Things that we all just need to move away from at some point. Same city. Same university. Parents."

"No girlfriend?" Sheilagh asked directly. She then blushed and smiled behind a hand. "I'm sorry," she said through her fingers. "I hope that's not too inquisitive."

I waved her apology away. "I did have a girlfriend. Her name was Helen."

Sheilagh looked into her coffee cup, stirring it lazily, following the spoon with her eyes.

"We broke up before I left," I continued.

"Why was that?" she asked.

"Just didn't love her," I said. "I mean, I did love her in a way, just not the same way she loved me, not the way she wanted me to love her."

Sheilagh looked up at me. "You mean she was pushing you?"

I shook my head. "No, not at all, but she did think I was running away from her by coming over here."

She fixed a look on me the same way she did that first day, smiling but with her head at an angle. "Do you still love her?" she asked slowly. "What I mean is, do you still hope it might work someday with her, this Helen?"

I didn't answer right away, just played with the sugar bowl. "I was actually quite fond of her," I said after a minute. "She's an accountant of all things."

Sheilagh fell silent for a few minutes and stirred her coffee thoughtfully. It was not an uncomfortable silence. After a bit she looked up and just smiled at me, an easy smile, heavy-lidded and content.

"What about you?" I said, finally. "Any boyfriends?"

"I am free at the moment." She refused to look up again, shy and flirtatious at the same time.

"Is that not expected to last?"

"Well, one never knows who might ring the bell out of the blue."

A waiter came by and offered us a dessert menu. We split a piece of bumbleberry pie and had some more coffee. Walking out the door after we'd finished, standing practically at the top of the hill, we could see the lights of Dundee shining to the north. Off to the east, in the Channel, we could just make out the flickering lights of the massive anchored rigs waiting to be towed to the rich oil deposits off the northeast coast. And seemingly right at our feet was the dim sooty glow of St Andrews, a few electric lights from the old town pulsing out weakly through the dark.

Sheilagh and I spent a lot of time together, often playing golf, but mostly just sitting around the house, watching TV, making jokes about the shows that were on, chatting about nothing in particular. Very few of our conversations had emotion as a topic, and if they did it was in talking about things past. We kissed briefly once, just as we were both going off to bed, and I pulled away after a few seconds.

"That was nice," Sheilagh said. She pecked me on the cheek. "I liked that."

I was reading in bed one night just two weeks before Christmas, a few days after we'd kissed. It had been a cold day and the house was frigid, so I had the blankets up around my neck. There was a soft tap on my door, just loud enough for an awake person to hear.

"Come in," I said. I sat up a bit and put a marker in my book. The door opened a crack and Sheilagh put her head inside.

"Hello," she said quietly. "Are you up?"

"Yes, yes," I said. "Come on in."

She came in and shut the door behind her. There wasn't really anywhere else in the room to sit so I waved my hand at the foot of the bed. A tiny smile crossed her lips and she sat gingerly beside my feet.

"What's up?"

Her hands were primly bundled up in her lap. "I'm sorry if I woke you."

I showed her my book and shook my head.

"Nothing's up, really," she said. "I just thought we might chat for a bit. I'm feeling rather talkative."

"Ahh," I said, slightly mimicking her. "Rather talkative, are we."

She asked me what I was reading. I read her a funny passage that she didn't laugh at, but then we laughed at the fact that she didn't find it funny. We talked about our roommates for awhile, and at one point she discreetly put her hand on my shin. My bedcovers were still between us, but she lightly ran her hand over the outline of my leg to my knee then back down to my ankle. She didn't look at my face, but followed her hand back and forth, back and forth, with that same tiny smile. She didn't speak, but I didn't think she wanted to say anything. After a couple of minutes I put my hand over hers. I held it and she looked up to me. Then she moved from the foot of the bed and came underneath the covers with me. We lay together for quite awhile before she undressed and we made love.

In a different age she would have defined physical beauty, the softness, the voluptuousness of her. She was generous and kind, but nervous with her touch. When I looked at her moving gently with my own movements, she had the same little smile, her eyes closed lightly, almost seeming to flutter. Her figure was so different from Helen's athletic boyish figure. I wondered as we made love who Sheilagh's other partners had been, if she ever thought of them, fantasized about them. I was conscious of wanting to please her, to make her know I thought she was beautiful.

She locked her fingers around the small of my back. I was close, and I bent my head to her ear and whispered her name. She said mine back, a bit louder, and then she said it again in a whisper to me.

Afterwards she fell asleep in my little bed, but she woke before dawn and put on all her clothes. I didn't try to persuade her to stay, and she dressed and left, going softly to her room so that our other roommates would not see or hear her.

I chose not to go home for Christmas. Sheilagh invited me to spend the holidays with her family in Glasgow, which I did. Her family were cheery and informal, and accepted me warmly into their house. I sent Helen a Christmas card but didn't get anything in return.

Sometime in mid-January Knellman left a note in my mail box saying a round of golf was in order to start the new year off right. The weather had been calm all through the holidays, and it had still been nice enough to play a few times a week, provided you wore your toque, but I didn't thrill to the prospect of playing with Knellman. I hadn't played with him since October. The time just prior to Christmas had been prickly. He was sniffing out a certain academic ambivalence on my part. Was I committed to history? he wanted to know. When was I going to have a clearer idea for a thesis? He would ask me such questions, sometimes even leaving them as notes in my mailbox, but he was impossible to reach when I thought he might be useful. And whenever we did meet he talked about nothing except himself, or some other topic he brought up only so that he could express an opinion on it. The thought of spending four hours alone with him on the golf course was sufficiently bleak that it occurred to me how problematic the next few years might be. I asked Gareth to play with us.

"Is he any good?" asked Gareth.

"Dreadful," I replied. "He's one of the worst golfers I've ever seen."

"Super," he said. "A right old wanker, too, no doubt."

"The worst."

"I can't really lie to you, Sean. This doesn't sound like much of a giggle."

"I know, Gareth, but I just don't think I could stand four

hours alone with him. He'd probably want to talk about my work."

Knellman was standing on the first tee waiting for us when we got there. He was wearing plus-fours with yellow socks, and had on a shirt and tie with a burgundy sweater over top. His cap was pulled low over his forehead. He nodded when I introduced him to Gareth, and kept both hands on his driver, waggling it.

"Can I expect the same thing from you out here as from Mr Fraser?" he asked Gareth.

Gareth laughed. "You can expect me to kick Sean's bony arse. That's about all."

"Right, then," he said, tersely. "Let's get round this course."

We insisted that he hit first. He lined up and talked as he did. "This hole calls for a hook," he said, saying it like kook. "Let's see about that."

He swung and missed the ball completely, thrashing wildly at it and launching a sizable chunk of turf in the process. After closely inspecting the face of the club for imperfections, he tried again and managed to stab it forty yards down the fairway just past the forward tees.

"Well in," said Gareth. Knellman looked at him and then shot a look at me.

Knellman became increasingly frustrated with his game as we went on. He began to curse the game before he even made contact with the ball, which was not always guaranteed. He would stand over the ball in a tense and rigid manner, make his backswing so slowly that he might have been protecting a tender shoulder, and then he would slash the club towards the ground as if he were viciously beating a dog.

"Christ!" he would roar, even before impact. The ball would squirt fifty or sixty yards in some unforeseen direction. Once, on the tee of the seventeenth hole, he nicked the ball at such a precise perpendicular angle with the heel of his club that it shot between his legs, just missing Gareth and me, and skittered back onto the sixteenth green, where the foursome behind us were putting.

"Fuck me backwards!" said Gareth with delight. "I've never seen that before." The foursome from the other green politely rolled Knellman's ball back, laughing jovially. He glared at the turf and didn't say a word for the rest of the round.

Knellman shook our hands after we putted out on the eighteenth green, and to my surprise insisted we join him for a drink back at his club, the New Club, one of the many private clubs near the course. Gareth shot me a panicky look but I couldn't say no, so we went.

The walls of the club were panelled with dark oak and had large paintings around the main room, most of them portraits of famous golfing figures. Old Tom Morris, the founder of the modern game. Young Tom Morris, his prodigiously talented son, who won the Open four times and died of sadness the day after his wife died in childbirth. Walter Hagen. A young Jack Nicklaus. The brilliant Spaniard, Seve Ballesteros. The room struck me as being historically more interesting than any of the books I'd read or the papers I'd written since I'd arrived.

We all ordered a pint, and Knellman had a scotch with it.

"Well!!" he said magnanimously, rubbing his hands together. "That was a jolly good round. Thanks to both you young men. A splendid round of the grand old game, eh!? Jolly good!"

Gareth squinted at him. "You don't mean to say that you like the game."

"Like the game? Young man, I love the game. No other game matches the demands of golf. A man must surely know who he is on the golf course, or the game will expose his flaws. Don't you agree, Fraser?"

I choked on my pint. "Without question, Dr Knellman."

"That sounds like a load of shite to me," said Gareth. "You hit the ball, find it, and hit it again. You don't need to think."

Knellman stayed silent just long enough to make it clear that he was assessing Gareth. "A simple philosophy," he finally said.

"But obviously an effective one. You play a lovely game. You don't need to think, you say. Perhaps your friend, Fraser, here, has taken such a philosophy too much to heart with his studies."

"Excuse me!?"

Knellman looked at me and pulled on his eyebrow. "Well, you must admit, Mr Fraser, that your academic performance to this point has been somewhat, shall we say, chequered."

Gareth claimed the need for a trip to the bathroom and fairly sprinted for it.

"Dr Knellman, I don't think this is the right time or place for you to be assessing my academic performance. In front of my friends. In a bar."

"Anytime I deem it necessary is the appropriate time to discuss your academic performance."

"I don't agree."

"Very well, then. Don't. But you had better make a decision young man, as to whether or not you want to be a historian. Your work has been lax. No commitment. Whether you stay or go is of no consequence to me at this point. I will not allow substandard students to tarnish my reputation."

"Well, you haven't been much help. The only time I see you is when I run into you in the hallway."

He brushed me aside. "I can be found if needed. This is the British way. Not like the babysitting you Americans want."

Without even finishing his drink he got up and left. Gareth came back a few minutes later.

"What's that wanker's problem?"

I shook my head. "How do I know."

"Needs a fucking good crack on the head, he does."

"That prick!" I said, suddenly angry. "The gall of the man. I'd listen to him if I had an ounce of respect for him, but he's just a prick with a Ph.D. Some fucking help he's been."

Gareth took a sip of his pint, and looked over at me. "Very nice lager, this. If we've got his tab, perhaps we should do another."

"Absolutely," I said, fuming. I signalled to the barman for two more.

Gareth leaned over towards me. "Hey, don't take it so hard, old man. All in a day's work. Look, let's down these and go play another nine holes. That'll cheer you up."

"Not likely," I said. "I should have told the asshole what I thought of him."

"Plan A for tomorrow."

I laughed. "I don't think so. Then I'd be out for sure."

We finished off our pints and just as we got near the door the barman brought us a bill.

"Gentleman told me you weren't to put anything on his tab. Sorry, lads."


On the first of March a Russian tanker passing through to Leningrad ran aground right on the edge of the estuary. It had been following the shoreline in a bad late February storm and fouled on a deep-water ridge. The locals claimed the next day that any sailor should have known the ridge was there and had been there for hundreds of years. The tanker was in no danger of sinking, but it was listing badly and had its nose pointed right into town. The Russian sailors came into St Andrews and Dundee while they waited the two days for enough tugs to arrive from Edinburgh. The whole town walked along the beach and the pier to get a look at the tanker sitting there like a massive metal iceberg. It was an event.

Also on the first of March I got a letter from Helen. The first communication I had received from her. Sheilagh wasn't home when the mail came. I took the letter up to my room, and sat on my bed while I read it.

Her parents were divorcing. Her mother had been seeing someone else, someone they all knew, and had just up and left the family. Helen's father was devastated, as was Helen. She still loved me, she said. She wasn't exactly counting on me ever being back, but she wanted me to know about her life. It sounded like she meant it, that she still loved me.

I sat on my bed for an hour or so, reading the letter over and over again. After folding it back into its envelope, I put it into the book I had on my small night table, and used it as a mark. When Sheilagh came home after an evening class, I was sitting in the living room, with a blanket on my lap, watching TV.

"Hello," she said gaily. "What are you watching?"

"Snooker."

"Is it exciting?"

"Snooker!?"

"Well, then," she said, looking at her watch, then pushing her lips out. "We're alone. We could do something else."

I looked over at her. "Like what?"

She grinned and seemed embarrassed. "Not if you don't want to. But, well...we could if you wanted to."

I threw the blanket off my lap and we went up to her room. We stopped once or twice on the way to kiss, and I stroked her head as we went up the stairway. Right after we finished I touched my lips lightly to both her cheeks, then her forehead, and went back to my room.

Lying in bed I picked up a text I'd promised to discuss with Knellman the next day. He'd said he wasn't going to speak to me unless I finished the book, but it was as likely he wouldn't show up at all. I put the book down ten minutes later. I picked Helen's letter out of my other book but didn't read it, just looked at it for a few minutes before putting it back.

Two days later, Sheilagh wanted to go down to the pier to see the tanker get towed off the ridge where it had run aground. The tugs had arrived the night before, but it was too dark to work by the time they had finished having a few pints with the Russians.

The pier, the beach, and the seawall were packed with people.

The tugs were drifting around the tanker like flies circling a cow, attaching ropes here and there. Finally there was a move in the same direction by all the tugs at the same time. The ropes attached to the tanker went stiff as rods. Nothing seemed to happen for a long time, a few minutes at least, before the angle the tanker sat at visibly changed. It actually bobbed and then found its water mark. The tugs blasted their horns and the beach erupted with cheers. One of the tugs had a fire hose, and it sprayed water high in the air. The tanker let out a deep bellow through its horn, a sound so loud you could feel it through your chest.

"Look at that!" said Sheilagh. "That is amazing. How did all those little things move that big huge thing!"

The tugs dropped their ropes and distanced themselves as the tanker fully righted itself. It blasted its horn three times and everybody cheered again. I stayed quiet.

"Isn't that brilliant!" said Sheilagh, clasping her hands together and then unclasping them to wave to the now-departing tanker. There were hundreds of people along the seawall and beach. It was a sunny calm day and everybody was waving and cheering even though very few of the Russian crew were on deck. The tanker, turning its huge bulk at an almost glacial pace, got its nose pointed towards the Continent and then it started for home.

## THE Q BALL

I went to meet my father at Pearson Airport on a Saturday morning in February. We said hello and shook hands. After scanning the empty luggage wheel for his bag, he turned back to me. "So here I am to check up on you," he said, cocking his head in a friendly way.

I nodded at him. "Glad to have you here."

Looking around distractedly he patted his coat pocket. "I wouldn't mind a cigarette," he said. The new smoking laws, which he thought unconstitutional, had just come in.

The luggage wheel made some grinding sounds and we both turned to it, but the chute produced nothing. I snuck a look back to my father. Prunes of skin hung under his eyes. He was a thin-faced man, always impeccably shaven, but he looked tired, probably because he was such a nervous flyer, as was my mother. My parents had worked and retired in Victoria, and he'd decided to come out to Toronto only two weeks ago, a rashly impulsive act for him.

"Too bad Mom couldn't make it," I said.

"Winter wings," he said, without looking back to me. "She doesn't trust those guys to de-ice them properly. She says they make six dollars an hour, and how can you trust your life with someone who makes six dollars an hour."

"There's a good point," I said.

Finally his bag came tumbling out of the chute like a bale of hay, and he stepped in front of some woman and dashed along the wheel to retrieve it. "Here, let me take that," I said, when he came back to where I was standing. I took his bag from him and slung the strap over my shoulder. He reached inside his chest pocket as we hit the door and pulled out his cigarettes.

When we got back to my house I brought my father into the living room. One of my four roommates, a musician from Newfoundland named Donald, came drifting shirtless out of the bathroom. He was built like a popsicle stick and his white boxer shorts billowed out of his open fly. He was clearly very badly hung over and the way he dragged the back of his hand across his mouth made it look like he'd just been throwing up.

"Lord!" said Donald, quickly buttoning up his fly. I introduced my father. Donald wiped his hand on his jeans and thrust it out. My father took it without hesitation, something, knowing Donald, I would not have done. He sat down with us for a few minutes then got up to leave.

"Where's everybody else?" I asked him.

He shrugged. "Dunno. I just got up."

After Donald left I showed my father up to my room on the second floor of the three-story house.

"Where are you going to sleep?" he asked.

"The couch downstairs."

For a minute I thought he was going to insist he take the couch, but he put his bag in the corner. "Small room for three-ten a month." He went over to the window and looked out. "Is that smoke? What is that? A factory?"

I walked over to him. "Here," I said. "Give me your coat."

He took it off and handed it to me. I walked over to my closet and put it in.

"Your mother's upset you're not coming back west this summer." I had taken a summer legal aid position, in between years of law school, and it was going to be my first summer away from home. "She's worried you're slipping away from her or something."

"I'm sure she'll manage," I said, slouching against my desk. "Besides, she's got you to keep her company."

He turned and looked back out the window. He had a neat coin of baldness on the crown of his head but otherwise had thick grey hair. He was wearing a sweater vest over his shirt and there were small tufts of wool balled up along his collar, which fit loose around his thin neck. There was something outside he seemed to be staring at and he touched a hand to the window pane. "You should know," he said after a moment, "that your mother and I are having some troubles."

I lost my smile. My parents were one thing to me, not two things. I ran my fingers through my longish hair. It felt greasy. I had no idea what to say to him, and at that moment was unsure I even wanted to know about it.

"Troubles," I finally said.

He took a moist and unsteady breath. Still facing the window he didn't say anything for a long time. His eyes focussed on something outside, his fingers pushed and tested the glass of the window.

I let him get unpacked. He wanted to have a shower and while he did I sat in the living room brooding about what he'd told me. What did he mean by troubles? Was this something they were not going to be able to work out? I was suddenly scared of these questions, of the answers. I wanted them to resolve this privately and be done with it. I wanted them to just be what they always were.

By the time my dad finished and came downstairs it was past lunchtime. I had no food in the house so I suggested we walk up to Danforth Avenue and grab something. We were putting on our coats when he asked me about my godfather.

"When was the last time you talked to Carl?"

"Carl?" Carl had known my mother first and became friends with my father only during my parents' courtship. He'd known Carl thirty years now.

"Do you ever think to call him?"

I started to button up my shaggy overcoat. "I talked to him before Christmas. November maybe."

"You should call him more than that, you know."

"Every time we make plans he doesn't show."

My father turned to face the door, involved, it seemed, in an internal struggle.

"Pool two times ago," I continued. "Dinner last time. He didn't show up either time."

"I'll phone him," my father said, turning back around.

I shrugged. I didn't much like Carl. He'd been a big part of my childhood, or at least had been around for a lot of it, but his manner of living was radically different from mine. He drank hard and still pretended to a level of familiarity that hadn't existed between us since I'd been in junior high school. He'd quit all kinds of jobs, lived with half a dozen women after divorcing my godmother, moved around, and ended up in Toronto ten years back, driving a subway train with the TTC. Every time I saw Carl he would tell me about someone who'd jumped off a platform in front of a train he'd been driving. The highlight of each suicide seemed to be that he got time off work for it.

My father went back into the kitchen where the phone was. I took off my coat and followed. He dialled a number he knew by heart.

"Carl!" he said loudly, though with not much glee.

A loud stream of noise came from the other end of the line which lasted at least thirty seconds.

"I promised I would," said my father, cutting into the flow, which started again as soon as my father completed his utterance.

"Two, three days maybe," my father said. He nodded. "Yes, Alec does need checking up on." Pause. "I don't know. You'd have to ask him why he never calls." He made a face at me and then listened for another couple of minutes. "No, no...that sounds great, Carl. Great."

He hung up and turned to me. "He says you stood him up last time you agreed to meet for a game of pool."

"The liar!" I said. "I was there cue in hand."

"Anyway, he wants to meet at the same place tonight at seven. The Q Ball?"

It was a twelve-table hangout. You could drink while playing, which appealed to Carl. I liked pool but would rather have just gone to a movie or something with my father. It was too late now to suggest that. We put our coats back on and went to get some lunch.

Despite the cold, Danforth Avenue was sprawling with people shopping and strolling, picking up their vegetables and videos, papers and coffee. My father found walking tricky on the icy sidewalks and he complained about the weather. We had a souvlaki and he bought me groceries. The whole time he said nothing about he and my mother. I don't know if he was waiting for me to ask but I didn't want to.

Walking back to my house with the groceries, we went through Withrow Park, a rolling space that took up a few city blocks. From the higher ground on the east end of the park you could see the downtown core, off across the Don Valley. The chill air was starting to cut through my old coat and I wanted to get home but my father stopped to look at the skyline. An ochre soup of pollution fringed the ears of the taller buildings, and despite the heavy air all the buildings were visible.

"That is something," he said, looking off to the towers in the distance. He paused for a minute. "I could manage living here."

"You're not moving here, are you?"

He chuckled. "Don't sound so worried." He dropped his cigarette butt on the ground and extinguished it with his toe. We didn't say anything for a few minutes, just stood looking at the ragged beautiful skyline. It was an impressive modern sight.

"So," my father finally said, reaching for another smoke. "Why aren't you coming back home?"

I didn't say anything at first, because it struck me only then that he and my mother might actually have been concerned about why I wasn't coming back, that they might have wanted me back and were not just applying themselves to some parental duty.

"I don't know," I said. "I just want to stay here. Make some contacts. No major reason, I guess."

He nodded as I spoke. "What's that really tall one?" he asked, pointing to one of the massive bank buildings closer to the lakeshore.

I wrapped my arms around me as best I could while holding the grocery bags. "Can we go back," I said. "I'm freezing."

He looked back to me for a second. "Sure," he said, looking at my coat. "Sorry."

There was more activity in the house when we got back. Donald had gone back to bed, but my three other roommates, all of whom I liked and was looking forward to living with in the summer, were around. I introduced them to my father, then he and I sat in the living room watching golf on TV for a couple hours before he went for a nap. When he got up I made him dinner with the groceries he'd bought me. After eating and cleaning up, having lost track of the time, we had to rush to meet Carl and took a cab instead of the subway.

The Q Ball was a middle-brow hall not too far from Chinatown. Carl already had a table and was shooting by himself when we got there. He was halfway through what I assumed was his first beer. We walked over and when he saw us he put his cue on the table.

"Jeremy!" he said enthusiastically, grabbing my father's hand. They shook for a minute and then Carl turned to me. "Alec, buddy!" he exclaimed, slapping me noisily on the shoulder. "Damn, it's good to see both you two. It's been a coon's age."

"Longer," said my father.

Carl nodded appreciatively. "That's the sorry fucking truth."

After getting some beer we got down to playing pool. We racked the balls and I broke, fluking the two-ball. Then I ran five balls before scratching in off the eight-ball on an unlucky kiss.

"Look at that little shit, will ya!" exclaimed Carl gleefully. "Great stroke!"

My father nodded. Carl had always done this, praised me excessively, though he did it only when my father was around. When I was a kid I liked the fulsome praise, but didn't now. I had no idea what my father made of it.

Carl took a big swig of beer and made quenched thirst sounds. "A beer and some pool. On a Saturday night." He took another sip and put his beer down, then said nostalgically, "Saturday... Saturday used to be hump day."

My father made a practised laugh, like he'd heard the line before.

We played a few games, making the odd shot, missing more than we made. Carl was a good player and got on one or two nice runs. In the middle of a run he stopped and openly leered at an attractive but heavily made-up woman about my age who walked by our table. He stood and held his cue near the tip, resting it on his large stomach, smiling at the woman as she walked by. She ignored him. Carl had two rings on each hand, chunky gold and gem creations. He also wore a dangly gold wrist bracelet. The woman walked to the other end of the hall. Carl watched her all the way and then turned back to us.

"I get these fantasies, sometimes," he said conspiratorially. "I'm just driving the subway, late at night, last run. A woman, like that one, younger than me and just fuckin' stacked, comes up to the driver's cab and opens the door. She comes in and stands behind me. And she just starts touching me. You know? She touches my head. Runs her hand down my arm. She runs her thumbtip, like this, around the rim of my ear. It's not even sexual." He paused. "Well, not always. But it's like she's there for me, with me. She understands me. That's it. She understands me."

"I'm going to start riding near the driver," I said.

Carl grinned at me. He looked back to the table and surveyed the position of the balls with great care, bending over, checking lines and angles. He did this with every single shot, as if there were something at stake. After hitting a shot he said offhandedly to my father, "How's Dorothy?"

My father waited a minute. "You're lonely," he finally said, his tone more harsh than consoling. "That whole fantasy of yours is just being lonely."

Carl stood up from the table and looked at my father. He rested the tip of his cue on the green baize of the table. "Maybe I am," he said. "But who isn't?"

I thought my father might say, "Not me," but he didn't. He didn't say anything. He just watched Carl, not even seeing if Carl dropped any balls but just following him around the table with unblinking eyes. I noticed for the first time how much my father was sweating. Moons of perspiration were setting under his armpits, creeping down his shirt.

"Take your sweater off," I said to him. "You look hot."

He ignored me, and lit a cigarette while watching Carl shoot.

Finally Carl missed a shot. "You silly fucker," he said under his breath. "Left 'er in the jaws." He moved off the table. "Hey!"

he said to me. "Hey, shooter! You're up." He walked over and stood beside my father.

I went up to the table and sank a ball, but the cue ball came to rest against the far cushion. I chalked up and meandered down the length of the table. It's not what you make, they say, it's what you leave, and I'd left myself nothing. Standing at the far end I saw Carl and my father close to one another. They were speaking, softly but urgently, and kept their eyes on the table.

I had no shot and made a feeble stab at curling the cue ball over to a target ball by the side pocket. I shanked it and scratched into the far corner pocket. I smiled as I stood up and looked across the length of the table to my father and Carl. They were facing each other now, cues in front of them. I started to walk over to that end of the table, and as I did I began to pick up the conversation.

"That's old news," Carl said dismissively. He was still holding his cue with both hands, my father held his in one hand.

"Not to me," my father said.

Carl let out a sort of derisive laugh. "Well, whose problem is that?"

"I'm telling you it's your problem."

I got over to where they were. "Dad," I said. "Your shot." He didn't hear me.

"Talk to your wife," said Carl. "Not me."

"I have," my father said curtly.

"Didn't hear what you wanted to hear, eh?" Carl said, laughing. He seemed to be almost enjoying, even purposefully escalating, my father's agitation, and he started walking over to the small round felt-covered table our beers were on. Carl didn't see that my father was coming to boil, which surprised me considering how long they'd known one another. But I could see it. I could see my father's face going splotchy. He reached out and grabbed Carl hard by the upper arm. He was taller than Carl, but Carl was a thick-set man.

The grab stopped Carl. He turned, somewhat theatrically. "What is this?" he asked, shaking off my father's hand. "Don't fuck with me like that, Jeremy."

"I'm not done talking," said my father, his voice trembling.

"Do I give a shit?" Carl asked impatiently. "This is bullshit." He turned around again to walk away and my father picked up his pool cue by the butt end with one hand.

"Carl," he said quickly, starting to walk after him. Carl didn't turn, but was only a step or two in front. With no further warning my father raised his cue like a riding switch and slashed it through the air. The thin end came down across Carl's head near his ear and over the side of his face, making a sharp cracking sound. Carl screamed and fell heavily, his cue clattering on the wooden floor. The noise attracted the attention of most of the other people in the place. A few of them came running over, thinking it was some sort of accident.

"Oh my God!" I hissed. "Dad!" He was still holding the cue in the air. I reached out and put my hand around it, and the instant I did so, he let go and took a step to the side, nearer the table. Carl was squirming on the floor, making a stunted groaning noise. He had both hands clamped to his head.

"What are you doing?" I said hoarsely to my father. "Jesus Christ!"

He didn't say anything but stood looking at Carl.

Carl picked himself up with one hand still on his head and stood leaning against the table. The other patrons stood gaping at us like people caught in a stick-up, stiff-armed, waiting to be told what to do next. Carl moved his hand to the base of his ear and gingerly probed at it, working his jaw subtly at the same time. A fat purple welt had risen across his cheek in a straight line from ear to nose, a blue spot of chalk dusted his nostril. He noticed the people. "Go away," he told them flatly. Instantly, relievedly, they moved off.

Holding my father's cue like a beefeater with a pike, I stood almost exactly between him and Carl. What connected them in the past had snapped, and something else was there in its place, something thinner, sharper. I could feel it taut in the air between them, strung now without elasticity or forgiveness.

"Are you okay, Carl?" I asked, though I did not step towards him.

He nodded at me, then looked over to my father. "That's what you came for?" he asked huskily. It looked like it hurt his face to talk.

My father started to fidget a little. He was coming down off his adrenaline. I looked over at him, but he refused to meet my eye and kept staring at Carl.

Carl pushed himself off the table, a little unsteadily, and looked first to my father, then over to me. "Later, sport," he said. He walked to the wall and took his coat off the hanger. Before he left he stopped at the till and put down some money. I never saw Carl again.

My father told me that night he would be leaving the next day. I don't know if he'd booked his flight that way, or if he had to purchase a new ticket. Over breakfast the next morning at a café down the street from me, before he caught his cab, I tried to talk to him about him and Carl, but he was unwilling to go into any detail.

"What did all this have to do with Mom?" I asked.

"Nothing now," he said.

"So it was something years ago?" I hesitated to state openly what I thought it had to be, unsure of how it would sound coming out of my mouth, and of how he would react.

He stirred his coffee, lit a cigarette. "What do you really think of Carl?" he asked, placing his cigarette in the ashtray. "Truthfully."

I frowned. "Well," I hesitated, "I didn't mind him when I was younger."

He nodded, had a sip of coffee, looked out the window. "I'm sorry," he said finally. "I'm sorry you saw me like that." He was not emotional, but he wouldn't look at me. His cigarette smouldered in the ashtray for a few minutes before he ground it out.

After finishing law school I stayed in Toronto. I ride the subway twice a day and habitually look for Carl in the driver's cab of every train, but have yet to see him. My parents are still together, older and slower now, living a quiet life in Victoria. They seem happy. I don't think my mother ever found out what happened at The Q Ball. I never mentioned it, and who knows what, if anything, my father told her.

Every summer I visit my parents for a week, ten days maybe. I help in the garden, take them out for a meal or two; we talk a little but not much. I have been tempted on occasion to ask my father, or even my mother, about Carl, but knowing will not make me love them any more or any less, so I leave it alone. I'm not uncomfortable around them and am happy for the time I spend with them.

But I'm also happy when I get into a seat on a plane heading back east, though I have inherited from my parents bad flying nerves. I just find it so hard to understand how those massive things get and stay airborne, though somehow they do. Take-offs are the worst. Lights flash above my head. I close the seatbelt over my waist. The plane shudders then shoots down the runway. The front tire lifts off the sticky tarmac. After that it's all I can do to close my eyes and hang on until we level off.

▲▲▲▲▲▲

# ANGLE OF INCIDENCE

Patty, my sister, is ten years older than me. She has a husband and a new baby. I'm an uncle for the first time, our parents new grandparents. They hadn't yet seen Kyla, who is two months old, so Patty arranged to fly out from Calgary to Toronto for a visit, and then return with our mother. Barry, Patty's husband, decided not to go to Toronto, glumly claiming a lot of pressure at work. He's a manager at some oil and gas company, his star apparently on the rise if what Patty tells me is true.

So it ended up being just me and Barry in their brand new house perched atop one of northwest Calgary's sprawling treeless suburbs, high on the foothills looking down the funnel of the city as it spilled eastward onto the prairie. They were letting me stay in their house rent-free during my last year of school, and all they ever asked of me was that I do my share of the dishes and housework. Patty had been married to Barry two years, and I wasn't certain I would have characterized my relationship with him as friendly, but I was close to my sister and was pretty sure she liked having me around.

After dropping Patty and Kyla off at the airport early on a Saturday night, Barry and I drove back to the house through a mild prairie snowfall, the kind of dry snow that seems light and full of nothing while it's falling, but you wake up in the morning to find your house buried in it.

"What are you up to tonight?" he asked me as he zipped into the garage. He always liked to open the garage from halfway down the block so he could shoot into it like it was the Batcave.

"No plans," I said. "I thought I might go down to the library."

He shut off the car almost before it had come to a stop. "I've got this work thing to go to."

"Oh yeah."

"I've got to make an appearance. It's kind of a stag." He shook his head, like he knew it was going to be a waste of his time. "One of the managers from work is getting married next week."

"In February?"

"Why not," said Barry, running a hand through his thick black curly hair. "Good time to pick up a ball and chain."

I let that pass, unsure if he was joking. Barry had a saturnine manner, though when the mood was on him he was capable of being funny, in a dark kind of way. He had a low infectious laugh, but didn't laugh very often.

"If you come with me it'll be easier to leave early, like we have to meet Patty later or something," Barry said. "We can grab a pizza or something first."

"You don't seriously think I want to go to this thing?"

"It won't be so bad," he said, closing the garage door behind him as we went inside. "Come on."

It was hard to say no, given that I was living in his house for free.

"All right," I said. "But I do want to get some work done tonight."

"Good man," he said, as I turned and went downstairs to

change.

We went to The Parthenon, just off Crowchild Trail, and when we got our food I asked Barry if he liked being a dad so far. "It's all right," he said, talking as he chewed. "There are ups and downs to everything. Patty's pretty excited about it."

"Not you?"

"Yeah," he said, examining a mushroom before putting it in his mouth. "Sure."

"Well, that's good," I said. "You'd hate to do anything like that without being sure."

He looked at me like he didn't appreciate being teased, though I wasn't teasing him.

"So who is this guy? That the stag's for."

He shrugged.

"What's his name?"

"Roy, I think."

Barry was not the easiest person to be in a conversation with, so I just sat back and decided to let him carry the ball for awhile, which he didn't. We finished our pizza and drove over to the stag pretty much in silence. The snow was still coming down, gently but insistently, and I knew I'd be shovelling in the morning. Once or twice I looked over at Barry. He was concentrating on the road, his heavy brow wrinkled like he was thinking about something he didn't want to be thinking about. He was coughing a lot, forcing it out, though he didn't seem to have a cold.

"You getting a cold, or what?" I asked.

He looked over at me, then back to the road. "Why?" he smirked. "You worried about catching it?"

We pulled up in front of an oilmen's club, which was infamous for only recently having allowed women to join. There was a large open lobby with a bulletin board announcing which function was in which room. All the rooms were named after cattle. Hereford House. Charolais Court. Simmental Hall. We scrolled down the list and saw Barry's party.

NorthStar Oil and Gas—The Holstein Room.

The coat check was off to the right, underneath a curving stairwell. When we checked our coats, the young woman said, "Shall I put both on the same hanger?" She had a name tag that said Charlotte on it.

"Sure," I said. "Does it matter?"

She shrugged and smiled, and when she did the corners of her eyes crinkled. "No," she said. "Not to me. But some of the gentlemen, particularly the older ones, are fussy about that sort of thing." She looked a little older than me, and I thought I recognized her from around university, but couldn't be sure.

"Come on," said Barry abruptly. "Let's get this over with." He started up the stairs.

I smiled back at Charlotte and she cheerfully waved the fingers of one hand. "Have fun."

The Holstein Room was big enough to accommodate a kind of dance floor, a small stage, and ten tables with eight chairs at each. It was about 9:30 when we went in. There was a man selling liquor tickets just inside the door. Barry bought four. After he handed Barry his change, the ticket man asked us if we were interested in entering the draw for the door prize. Barry said no without asking what the prize was and went inside.

The tables looked full, but someone shouted Barry's name and motioned for him to come over. The men at the table were mostly older than Barry and some looked at least twice his age, maybe even closing in on retirement. I was immediately aware, as everyone else in the room must have been, that this was a table for the company big shots. They'd saved one chair, but as soon as they saw he had someone with him, they made a big deal about getting another chair for me. When I had a seat and everyone else was back at the table, Barry introduced me.

"This is Malcolm," he said. "Patty's little brother." I tossed a look at him, but said nothing, just turned back to the grinning inebriated faces now reciting their names for me.

One of the older gents who'd saved Barry a seat beside him sat rubbing his chin. His name was Arthur. He was on the short side, had glasses and thinning hair, and looked like a nice enough guy. "Malcolm," he said, ruminating like it was a name he had a personal attachment to or fond memory of. "Sounds queer," he concluded dryly. The others at the table laughed. One of them slapped me fraternally on the back while I fidgeted with my glasses.

Barry and I ended up on different sides of the table. He held up his drink tickets. "Beer?" he said. I nodded. He was back in a few minutes, and passed me my unopened beer as if it were a baton.

"Thanks a lot," I said, twisting the cap off. None of the others were listening, and didn't catch my tone.

Suddenly the whole gang of them burst into hysterics. "Hey, Barry," said one of the younger of the group, who was still clearly older than Barry. "Why are women like Listerine?"

Barry looked over at him, smiling. "Why?"

"Because," the man said, barely able to contain himself. "You hate 'em, but you still use 'em!!"

Everybody howled again. Barry laughed along with them.

Where I was sitting, I had my back to the wall. Arthur, the man who had poked fun at my name, got Barry in to a private conversation. They bent their heads bent close together. Arthur was doing all the talking and Barry the listening. Barry stared at the table and nodded a lot. Arthur had thick hands and stubby fingers, and he gestured freely, confidently, while he talked.

No one at our table seemed particularly interested in talking to me so I surveyed the room and tried to figure out who the groom was. Up at the front, near a podium, there was a table noisier and more populated than the others. One man was slumped in his chair. He was grinning, but looked more trapped than anything. He seemed the centre of attention.

A stiff elderly man at our table made a show of checking his watch and then went to the podium, mounting the steps a little unsteadily. The guy sitting beside me leaned over and said conspiratorially, "That's Morten Macon, the CEO." The man's breath smelled of beer and salsa, and seemed worse because he was whispering. "He's an asshole."

Morten Macon got everyone's attention and asked Arthur to come up, describing him as "everybody's favourite senior VP and my trusted 2IC." There were muffled guffaws from some of the other tables.

I leaned back to the guy beside me. "2IC?"

He looked at me with slight disdain. "Second in command."

Arthur was heavy into his conversation with Barry and disengaged himself by waving a pointed finger. "Think about that," he said to Barry. "I'll be back." Barry took a swig of beer. He looked frustrated about something.

Arthur strode to the front of the room and took the podium. "Thanks, Morty," he said casually, embarking on a toast to the groom that involved numerous jokes and slanders against the gender he described as being "nearly, but thank God not totally, without representation this evening." This drew snickers from certain members of the crowd.

"I can safely say," he said, at one point, with no indication he was trying to be funny, "that the only thing I've learned from my three loving and blissful unions is that marriage is a lot like a tornado." He paused to let us consider the wisdom of this. "At first, there's a lot of sucking and blowing, and then you lose your house." The crowd erupted.

After about another ten minutes of the same he concluded by saying that this was the groom's last week of freedom and to that end, the hat had been passed around at work to provide him with a going away present to remember. Arthur signalled to a man at the back of the room, who knocked on the door of some sort of back room, a cloakroom, or kitchenette.

Arthur left the podium and came back to his seat beside Barry. The other men at our table stood up, but Barry and Arthur did not.

The door of the back room opened and a young woman came out. She was wearing almost nothing, cowboy boots and hat, a g-string, nipple tassels. She had bright hair, almost a copper colour, that draped across her naked back and hung almost as far as her hips. With her toe she switched on the ghetto box at her feet, and the sound of the Pink Panther theme filled the room. It was slinky music and she went from table to table pretending to look for the groom, but provocatively touching just about every man in her path as she made her way to the main table. Everybody was hooting and hollering, and the men standing beside the groom were pointing at him and shouting his name.

The other men at our table had gravitated towards the front of the room for the show, but Arthur and Barry stayed where they were, ignoring what was happening. Barry was saying no to something.

"I think you're possibly misrepresenting my position, Arthur," he said. "I'm not sure how comfortable I am with that."

Arthur picked up his beer and took a quick but measured swig. "I didn't ask if you were comfortable with it," he said, turning his gaze for a second to the scene at the front of the room. The stripper was circling the groom, rubbing her tasselled breasts against the back of his head. Arthur turned back to Barry and as he did he saw that I was in listening distance, which he seemed not to care much about. Barry was bent forward, holding his beer, his elbows on his knees. He was slowly shaking his head, almost in time with the slinky Panther music

"Did you even read my memo?" Barry asked him pointedly. Arthur nodded. "Yes, I did."

"And?"

"I don't see the problem," said Arthur.

"What are you talking about?"

"What are *you* talking about?"

"Look," said Barry. "Maybe there's a difference of interpretation here."

"I don't need to interpret anything," Arthur said sharply.

The volume of the stripper's music went up and we all looked over. She had the groom's shirt off and was rubbing his chest. He looked a little green, but kept trying to smile. Arthur turned back to the table. I pretended to keep on watching the stripper.

"You'd better think hard about this one, Barry," Arthur went on.

"It'll look bad."

"That's your opinion."

"That's not an opinion," said Barry, slowly shaking his head back and forth. I'd never seen Barry like this, though I couldn't quite say what was different about him.

"That's just your perception," said Arthur dismissively. "Why don't you just relax."

"It'll put me in a bad position, Arthur." Barry stared at the floor, looking downcast and angry at the same time.

Arthur turned his attention to the stripper, who was now naked except for her cowboy boots. Sitting on the groom's lap with her fingers entwined around the back of his neck, she was grinding her crotch into his lap and pushing her breasts into his face. This went on for about ten minutes, with the stripper doing everything she could to titillate the groom without actually performing a sex act. Arthur and Barry didn't move but seemed to have finished talking.

The throbbing saxophone of the Panther music was starting to give me a headache. I looked over at Barry and tried to catch his eye so we could leave, but he was looking at his hands. Arthur leaned over towards him and whispered something in his ear. Barry looked up at him and said, "You don't need to tell me that," and then got up to get another beer.

After Barry left for the bar Arthur stood up, gave me a brief dismissive glance, and went back up near the podium. He seemed to be waiting for something to happen, and when the stripper got off the groom's lap and gave him a big sloppy kiss—a risky move, I thought, given the groom's state—Arthur turned on the microphone and asked for everyone's attention.

"Hey!" he said. "Guys!" Everybody stopped and looked at Arthur. The stripper picked up her g-string and tassels and went to stand by the door she'd come out of, though she did not go back inside. She looked deeply bored when out of the centre of attention. I looked back at the groom. He'd obviously been force-fed alcohol all night, and was slumped over in his chair.

"Well, we've seen a great show here," said Arthur. "Now the door prize."

A couple of guys shouted at the top of their lungs, "Pick me! Pick me!" Arthur stopped them cold with a look, and the room went silent. There was no question he possessed an air of authority, one that seemed closely linked to rebuke. Even in this circumstance a stare was all it took for him to bring someone to order. "Jeremy," he said in a deep dramatic tone. "The box please."

A bald fat man made his way to the podium. The crowd parted for him. He was carrying a shoe box, holding it at arm's length as if it were an ecclesiastical object. When he arrived at the podium he held the box over his head and let Arthur reach into it. Arthur pulled out a slip of paper and read it to himself, seeming to relish what it said. He looked up, glanced at the paper again, then regally surveyed the room. "The lucky winner," he said, drawing out every word, "is Barry!!"

At first there was an intake of breath, then groaning, then laughter. I was excited at first, and looked around for Barry, wondering what it was he'd won. Then I remembered he hadn't entered. It was obviously another Barry, I thought, but Arthur picked my brother-in-law out of the crowd, over by the bar. He pointed at him. "There's the lucky man!"

I stood up and looked over that way. Barry was standing with his beer in his hand, looking baffled. I could tell what he was saying to the men around him, something to the effect that he hadn't even entered. But Arthur had the microphone and started to chant, "BareRee! BareRee! BareRee!" Soon everybody was chanting and pushing Barry towards the back room.

The stripper came over to where Barry was. She isolated him from the others and grabbed onto his hand, pulling him towards the door. Arthur kept up the chant over the microphone. Barry looked my way. We caught eyes and he motioned for me to come over, but I moved only slightly closer. He was protesting with the stripper, who was making a production out of getting him into the back room past Barry's co-workers. They were all laughing and cheering, and Arthur's voice was still ringing out in a chant of Barry's name.

"Look," Barry was saying. "I'm married."

"Perfect," she said, with obviously fake naughtiness, and moved around to push rather than pull him toward the back room. He seemed to give in, as though he'd made his point. Someone tousled his thick black hair, mussing it up. He ran a hand through it to neaten it, smiled nervously, and handed his beer to one of the guys near him. When the stripper had Barry inside the room, she bent over like she was picking a coin up off the floor and held that position for a few seconds. Everybody cheered and then she closed the door.

Arthur watched this from the podium with the satisfaction of a man coaching his son's hockey team. "Do us proud, Barry," he said loudly. He shut off the microphone, and stepped down from his perch.

I was too stunned to move at first, but soon left and went to the bathroom, where I sat on the toilet for no reason other than to be by myself. A couple minutes later, someone entered the stall beside me, fumbled for an eternity with the lock, and then began an almost baroque vomiting session. It sounded like he was pouring runny cement and he flushed the toilet two or three times. I went to the sink and washed my hands and face, and as I left the bathroom I turned around and saw the groom lurching from the stall.

Not wanting to go back to the Holstein Room, I went down to the lobby and sat on a couch against a wall. Men were milling around, moving in and out of the other rooms. My sister was in Toronto at this moment, probably asleep given the time difference. I remembered the first time Patty ever mentioned Barry. It was when we were all still living at home with Mom and Dad. One night at dinner she announced she had met the man she was going to marry.

"Barry," she said to us, as though the word itself signified the life ahead of her. He was big, tall, not really good-looking, but seemed to fill a room. I figured it was physical between them. Mom and Dad liked him, but only in the sense that he was uncontroversial, respectable and polite, and already in a successful career. They never had time to get to know him, because they moved not long after Patty and he got serious.

After I'd been sitting in the lobby for about fifteen minutes, there was an ebb in the traffic. The coat check woman, Charlotte, leaned out of her cubicle. "Are you feeling all right?"

"Sorry?"

"You don't look too great." She smiled gregariously, but I couldn't really see her eyes through her glasses. "One drink too many, maybe?"

"No," I said to her. "Just a little tired."

She kept smiling. Two men from the stag were coming down the stairs and went over to get their coats. They looked about Barry's age, maybe slightly younger.

"Shitty luck," one said to the other. "The odds actually weren't too bad." Both made noises of missed opportunity, sucking air in through the corners of their mouths. Charlotte handed them their coats with a friendly goodbye. They left her a generous tip and when they went through the door she turned back to me and smiled again.

"There'll be more down soon, I bet," I said.

"Really? How do you know that?"

I thought for a moment how to say it. "The draw for the door prize is over."

She made a little face, scrunching up her nose, then put on a smile. "You didn't win, I take it."

"No," I said. "I didn't win." I looked around the lobby. "How can you work in a place like this?"

She looked a bit insulted. "I don't see you running for the door."

"I'm just waiting here for my brother-in-law."

She put up her hands. "Whatever."

I was about to get up and go over to her, when Barry came down the stairs with the stripper. She was laughing girlishly about something and touched her hand to Barry's chest. He was laughing, too, but stopped when he saw me. The stripper had her coat and boots on, but when she hit the bottom of the stairs she went to the washroom off the lobby. Barry and I got to the coat check counter at the same time. Charlotte had watched them come down the stairs, and had retrieved our coats without a word. Barry took his coat and went to the men's room.

I saw that Barry hadn't tipped Charlotte, so I pried a five out of my wallet and put it in her dish. She looked at me as though she'd have been just as happy without it. The stripper came out of the washroom and left the building, passing in front of the lobby's large plate-glass front window. What had obviously been a wig had been removed; she had short black hair slicked back across her scalp. Her broad smile had evaporated and her thin lips looked the colour of raw meat. She looked weary, and much older than she had in the Holstein Room. As she walked to her car, she checked her watch. Barry came out of the men's room, and went straight to the door and out. I followed.

"Enjoy the rest of your evening," Charlotte said from her booth, not smiling.

I stopped for a second, then threw my coat on and left.

As soon as he got the car started Barry turned on the radio to a loud rock station. I kept quiet. The snow had finally stopped, but a lot of it had accumulated and it felt like we were driving on a soft carpet. We were about halfway home before Barry spoke.

"Nothing happened," he said, tightlipped.

The radio was so loud I wasn't sure I caught him. I reached over and turned it down. "What?"

"I said nothing happened." He was fiercely chewing a piece of gum, and the smell of mint filled the car when he opened his mouth. "We didn't do anything, all right. I had to go in there, but we didn't fuck. We didn't do anything." He worked the gum loudly and looked in the rear view mirror.

"How could you have won? You didn't enter."

He looked for a moment like he was going to answer me, but then just smiled bitterly and let out a long exhalation through his nostrils, shaking his head.

"What about that Arthur guy?" I said. "That's your boss, isn't it?"

He nodded but kept his eyes on the road.

"What did he want," I asked, "all that time he was talking to you?"

He was silent for a few seconds before speaking. "Thanks for helping me out," he said. "For coming to my rescue."

I made a face. "You expected me to do something?"

He didn't say anything, just drove. I could hear his teeth coming together at the front of his mouth as he chewed his gum. I looked at him once or twice more, but he ignored me. We got home and he went straight upstairs.

The next day was Sunday and when I got up around eight he was gone, in to work, I guessed. Much as I'd predicted the night before, the snow was a good foot deep on the driveway and sidewalk, so I pulled on my boots and got the shovel out of the garage. It was a bright morning and the sun seemed to be coming up out of the snow when I looked at it. I had to wear my sunglasses while I shovelled to keep my eyes from watering.

Five days later, just after dinner on a Friday night, Barry went to pick up Patty, Kyla and my mother at the airport. I was studying and when I came up from the basement mom and Patty kissed me. We all went into the kitchen. I boiled water for tea, and fished some of Patty's homemade muffins out of the freezer.

Patty had Kyla in her arms and was making some cooing noises. "Grandma and Grandpa sure loved having you visit, didn't they? Yes, they did." She looked up and smiled at us, then handed Kyla to Barry.

"Hey!" Patty said suddenly, her green eyes dancing. "You know what I did on the flight back?"

We all looked at her.

"I did what you always do," she said to me. "I went to the flight deck!" She was practically squirming in her seat she was so excited to tell us. "For the first time. It was awesome!"

"I told you," I said. I had always been addicted to views from great heights, and visiting the flight deck was the ultimate. "Isn't it cool."

"I was asking the pilots questions," she said, nodding enthusiastically. She moved her small hands like she was trying to bring forth the questions from her head. "For instance, What is it that keeps planes aloft? Do you know?" She looked at us, particularly at Barry. He shook his head no, and looked down at Kyla.

"The angle of incidence," she said, pleased with the terminology. "It's an aerodynamic principle called the angle of incidence. The wing," she continued, positioning her hands to demonstrate, "sits at an angle different from that of the plane. The way the air flows over the wing makes the pressure higher under it than over it, so that creates lift. That's what keeps it up."

"Unbelievable," I said, smiling with jealousy. "All the times I've visited the flight deck and I never heard anything like that."

"That's interesting," said Barry, looking at his watch. "By the way, I've got to go into work pretty quick here. Just for a few hours."

Patty didn't speak, just looked quietly at Barry, deflated. I looked over at him. He wasn't really even paying attention to any of us. Kyla had spit something up and he was wiping it away with a cloth.

"So," my mother said, quickly changing the topic. "What did you two boys get up to while Patty and Kyla were gone?"

Barry gave me a brief neutral glance.

"Just school for me," I said.

We all looked at Barry. "I was busy making a living," he said. There was a brief silence, then my mother started asking Patty questions about various baby issues. It was then I understood that Barry was not going to tell Patty about the stag and the stripper. Right up until that point I'd kind of assumed he would. I guess I didn't have much reason for thinking this, but I did. A thick coil of tension wound itself around my solar plexus, and I realized that if I told Patty, or if I didn't, I'd be letting either her or Barry down. After I thought about it for a minute it wasn't too hard to make a choice, and once I'd done so I felt better about things, much clearer as to where I stood in relation to Barry. And to Patty.

I kept my eyes on Barry until he pushed his chair out to go and saw that I was watching him. I looked down quickly but back right away. He was about to get up and hand Kyla back to Patty when Kyla gurgled and laughed a bit. Barry didn't so much smile as examine her with great curiosity. He bounced her up and down a little on his knee, and continued to gaze intently at her, as though he were searching for something and thought that that was where he might find it. The rest of us, my Mom, me, Patty, were only half there, half real, much as we had always been.

▲▲▲▲▲▲

# SUNFLOWERS

▲▲▲▲▲▲▲

"**I** mean, do you like death threats!?" Willa asked, her voice scratchy and emotional. I looked over at her. With no warning, the glass of scotch left her hand, clattered against the far wall of the kitchen, and broke when it hit the floor.

It was eleven o'clock in the evening. I rose from the table to clean up the broken glass and scotch. Up to that point Willa had been composed, in control, solid as a filing cabinet.

"What possible point could there be in going to work? It's not like you're the Secretary General of the UN! Or the Pope. You're not that vital to the well-being of the cosmos."

I moved to the garbage can with the shards, then sadly rinsed the cloth in the sink. It was good scotch.

"Answer me." She came to the sink and stood bent over it, her nightie away from her body like a sail.

"Willa."

"Don't Willa me," she said. "Don't!" She sat down at the kitchen table and began to cry.

I went over and put my arm around her. "Do you think maybe

you're overreacting?" I said.

She took my arm off her shoulder, and got up and left the room without saying another word to me. I went back to the sink and washed the scotch smell off my hands, then poured myself a glass from a cheaper bottle sitting on the counter. After I finished off my drink I had another, and then went to work.

In the morning, after getting back from work, I went into the kitchen. The three of them, Willa and our two sons, were there, eating breakfast. My sons stared at their food. Willa ignored me. I pulled a coffee cup out of the cupboard.

"Listen to this," I said as I sat down. I huddled over my coffee, trying for some mood. "Last night this guy phones in, Hank or Frank or something, and he's a rig pig, you know, an oil worker." I took a sip of my coffee. John and Keith, my two boys, looked from me to their mother to see if she was listening. She was looking out the window over the kitchen sink, tracing an eyebrow with the tip of her ring finger. My sons looked at their food.

"He starts telling me this story about a buddy of his in Iqaluit who planted sunflower plants there last summer, and they actually grew. They reached the point where they had those big droopy heads full of seeds, but then it hit midsummer. Twenty-four hour sunshine."

Willa put down her cup. "More coffee?"

I looked at John and Keith in turn. "Well, as I'm sure you know, sunflowers follow the sun. Their heads actually turn with the sun. And since the sun shines and goes around all the time in the north, the sunflowers just followed it and eventually twisted their own heads right off." I moved my forefinger in the air, like I was describing a halo, stopped, then looked at my wife. "I think I'll plant some sunflowers out back here this summer."

From across the table Willa sluiced the contents of her coffee cup at me. I ducked my head to the side quickly enough to avoid most of it.

John shot up out of his chair. "You two are just twisted, you know that!? You're both just warped individuals!" He pushed his chair in and left the room. Keith followed John, studiously avoiding our eyes. Keith was a thoughtful boy, and it hurt me to see him in retreat. Willa and I were left alone, with nothing but a messy floor and each other to look at.

"What is it with this fluid phase?" I said to her. "Tossing drinks around. Grow up."

"Oh, Michael," she said, standing up. "You are a treat."

Two days later it was a flagon of red wine spattered on the area rug in the dining room.

The following week she left me. It was one of those events that the sum of one's life from birth does not prepare one for. She simply came home and announced she'd made up her mind. She was going to stay with her sister Carol. Carol was a fine woman, a lawyer, who had chosen to remain single. I made a few feeble stabs at persuading Willa to stay, but she would not relent. She felt it would be best if she left.

"I just need some distance from you right now, Michael," she said in the front entry, getting ready to go to Carol's. "We're like magnets of opposite polarity, you know, repelling each other when we're too close."

"Magnets of opposite polarity. Is that right?"

She let out a long low sigh, exhaled with the purpose of suggesting that she bore a difficult and unenviable burden.

"What about John and Keith?" I asked.

She opened the door. "What about them?"

I pulled a face. "So I'm supposed to look after them? Some mother you are."

"They can look after themselves. You don't have to play pretend father."

"Thanks for that vote of support. Call when you feel depolarized."

She took a shot at smiling, then kissed me on the cheek. I made a show of shutting the door firmly, but went to the front room, and peeked through the curtains like a kid, watching her go.

I told John and Keith when they got home from school, and they responded with silence and grimaces before shuffling off to the TV room.

I am an insomniac. Sleep is a foreign language to me. I have had to learn it, practise it, internalize the translation of wakefulness to sleep. I do sleep but only in small amounts, and even the little I manage requires careful planning and concentration. This is one of the reasons I work all night.

It was about three weeks ago that the death threats started. I was doing my show when a nasal-voiced man phoned in to say he was going to kill me. That first call was on-air and I laughed it off, but since then the calls have been coming in every few days on the producer's line, which I answer at night, rather than the on-air number. The guy doesn't even want air-time. He just wants to let me know that he is going to kill me. It can't be the nature of the program itself. It's only classical music and the occasional phone call I'll put on-air if someone interesting rings up. I cannot fathom the source of the man's hate for me, even after I went back and listened to a couple of the threats recorded by the tech.

So I have remained at work despite the threats and have not yet told the police. That is why Willa is furious with me and has left our household.

She came by for dinner the day after she moved out. We had a regular camping party going, the boys and I, barbecuing up some burgers, dipping some nachos into salsa. I even let them have a beer though they're still a couple years short.

Willa came through the house into the backyard. She looked happy for a moment.

"Well, well," she said. "I don't believe my eyes. You may actually survive without me after all."

"Hey! Mom!" The boys jumped up and went over to her. They hugged briefly.

"Hi kids! Hey, why don't you two go in and get your thirsty mother a scotch. I hate that beer stuff." She smiled at them and they loped into the house.

"You should not be giving those boys beer," she hissed at me once they were out of earshot.

"We were having a good time."

She went over to the barbecue and lifted up the lid to see what was inside. "Is there enough for me?"

"Sure."

"Did you go to work last night?"

I nodded.

"And?"

I nodded again.

"How can you do it?" she asked. "How can you stand it?"

I walked over to the barbecue beside her and when I got there she moved over to the picnic table. I flipped the burgers around for a minute, then turned to her. When I did I caught a glimpse of the kitchen window; the boys were looking out at us.

"It's not a big deal."

"Not to you, maybe." She looked around like she wanted her drink.

"Why don't you just leave it, Willa? You're wrecking our lives. Trust me."

"Trust someone who doesn't care about his life? There isn't anything honourable about this, you know. It's not working with lepers. It's just radio."

"I like my job."

"What if he kills you? What then?"

"He's not going to kill anyone. He's just some pathetic guy who stays up all night and has nothing better to do than terrorize me."

"But what if he did? I mean, you'd deserve it. But what if he did? How would that feel?"

I took a swig of my beer. "That would be hard to say, seeing as how I'd be dead."

"Aren't you clever," Willa said, half to herself. She paused for a second to gather her thoughts, as if she wanted to say something nasty but decided to rise above it. "Well, that just tells me you don't want this anymore," she said, waving her hands around the yard and at the house. "That's all."

"That's not true," I said. "Besides, you're the one that moved out."

"Yes, well, I'm sorry I've been such an anchor all along. I didn't realize."

"Willa, don't feel sorry for yourself. You can come back anytime. You don't need to make a statement."

"Come back to a man who acts like this?" She stood up and distractedly checked the hamburgers. "These are starting to burn," she said.

The boys must have decided that we'd had enough time. They came outside with their mother's drink and another beer for me.

The truth was, the guy did kind of scare me. But something wouldn't let me stay home or even call the cops, and I didn't know what it was. And the more Willa badgered me the more determined I became. But to do what? I didn't feel particularly threatened, or that I was in any physical danger, though I might have been. And why was I worth threatening? I wanted to know. It seemed more important than anything else at the moment. There was some kind of opportunity involved, I could feel it. Maybe to find out something about myself, something I didn't know. A chance to learn something.

We had our burgers incident-free and then sat back in the yard with another drink. It was a fine evening; the sun was still bright and the air seemed light and dry, smelled nicely of brownish grass.

"So how's life without your mother?" Willa asked the boys good-naturedly.

"Well," said John. "You know." He was the more athletic of my sons, the more dynamic of the two. Girls liked him. Keith was the gawky scientist type, though he was terrible at science. He kept pens in his shirt pocket. He loved books, especially detective stories.

"Right," said Keith. They shifted in their seats and took drinks of their iced tea at precisely the same instant.

"They're depressed," I said.

"Because their father is suicidal. I don't blame them."

"That's a bit of an overstatement."

"Why don't you just jump off a bridge? You might survive that, too."

"So pragmatic. So much common sense."

"You say that like it's a disease."

"Could be," I said.

She looked at the boys, who were finished their iced tea. "Don't listen to your father. He's saying strange things."

I rubbed my forehead. "Stop, Willa."

"Do you actually want them to think what you're doing is right? To accept that not caring about us is okay?"

Keith looked up from his empty glass. "It sounds like you're mad about something else, Mom."

"She's mad at herself because she's not romantic or adventurous," I said. "Mad because she wouldn't do what I'm doing."

Willa looked into the yard. Her eyes got shiny, like little pickled eggs. The three of us men tensed up a bit, readied ourselves for it, but she kept everything on the table. She got up only to go in the house. A few seconds later we heard the front door close.

Later that night he phoned again, right near the end of the programme, while a long Elgar piece was playing. It was about five in the morning and the tech had just come in to prepare for the early morning show, so I wasn't alone. But I knew it was the loony right away.

"Hello, asshole," he said, then he cackled maniacally. "Surprised to hear from me?"

"No," I said. "Honoured."

"FUCK YOU!" he suddenly screamed in my ear. "Don't you be sarcastic. Fucking dee-jay."

"Why are you calling me?" I asked.

"Cause I hate Elgar," he said. He laughed again. "Get it?"

"Very good."

"How old is your mother?"

"Pardon me?"

"Your mother. How old is she?"

"She's dead," I said.

"Mine, too," he said. "She was a scraggy bitch."

"But a good mother."

"Every time you open your fucking mouth," he said, "it reminds of why I am so looking forward to getting the fuck rid of you. Honest to fucking God."

"Just to satisfy my own curiosity," I said. "What is it you have against me anyway? You've never really told me."

"You got a wife?" he said.

"Sure. I had a fight with her tonight because of you."

"Oh." His voice went softer. "Sorry." He paused for a second, and then asked quizzically, "Does she give head?"

"Jesus," I said, half to myself. I checked the run on the Elgar piece. Ten minutes left. I signalled to the tech on the other side of the glass that I had the loony on the line, using the standard circular motion of the index finger at the temple. He smiled, took a swig from a large green coffee mug, and made a rotation of his hand in the air. Tape it? I shook my head.

"Let me ask you one question," I said to the loony.

Silence.

"Why can't you just go kill someone else? Why kill me?"

He drew breath, seemed to hold it, and then blew out, like he was smoking pot.

"Hey, pal, we all got to kick it sooner or later. You might as well be sooner. It's fate, don't you think?"

"No, I don't think that at all."

"It's like a karma thing."

"Jesus, I'm being terrorized by a Moonie."

"Hey! Fuck you!" He seemed genuinely insulted, then said, "What's a Moonie?"

"You are so stupid," I said. "I should be scared of someone as stupid as you."

"You'd fucking well better be scared, numb nuts. Your meat is so close to being crispy I can taste it. It's inevitable."

"Right," I said. "So is this." I hung up.

I motioned to the tech that I was off the line and he made a brow-wiping motion. We laughed, but when I finished laughing I looked down at the drops scattered on the desk in front of me, sweaty little seeds released from my forehead, the febrile seeds of my fear.

I called Willa the next morning and asked her if she wanted to come over for breakfast. She was there in twenty minutes.

"My sister thinks you're being a jerk," she said, as soon as she had a coffee and was seated. "She agrees with me that you're being selfish and even adolescent, like it's some macho thing. Like you think that if you stay on going in that you'll overcome some kind of weakness in yourself."

"How is Carol?"

"She thinks it's a man thing."

I got up and put some pancakes and eggs over-easy on a plate for her, then fished the syrup out of the fridge. It was a gamble putting that in front of her.

"Willa," I said. "I have a suggestion."

She lifted her head up from the syrup and gave me a level

gaze. The syrup stopped flowing.

"Why don't you come in with me tonight?"

"To the station? Why would I want to do that? I don't want to get killed, too."

"Nobody's going to get killed. Come on. Why not?"

She eyed me suspiciously.

"Come on," I said. "I want you to come." I felt as though I needed to make some kind of gesture after the way she'd left the night before.

She finished pouring the syrup on her pancakes and started chewing thoughtfully. I knew then she'd come. She always was slower to agree than to disagree.

Willa met me at the studio at about 11:45 pm. We went in and got some tea from the staff lounge while the late show finished up. We didn't say much. Willa had applied just the slightest hint of makeup. I was touched by this small gesture. She looked soft and kind, sexy in a subtle self-assured way. Just before the midnight news feed from Toronto ended, the tech waved goodnight and left. Willa and I were alone.

My plan was to play long pieces all night in case the lunatic phoned. It was also a way to build in the occasional automatic timeout if Willa and I started to fight. I figured on a break every fifteen minutes or so.

"When does he usually call?" she asked during a Debussy piece.

"No set time. Most nights he doesn't call."

She swivelled in her chair slightly. "That must make you anxious. Sort of waiting for him to call."

I shrugged.

"So male," she said, looking at me sidewise. "Aren't you?" She swivelled around again in her chair, then started looking at knobs and switches and mikes.

"Do you really read all night when you're here?"

"It's wonderful. I turn the music down. It's quiet."

"Since you got this job, what, eight years ago, I have always fallen asleep listening to you. Or at least the program. Did you know that?"

I raised my eyebrows. "I always thought you were asleep by midnight."

"I used to be. But I like listening. Knowing you're there. It's a sort of security in itself, I guess."

"Do you need that security?"

"Don't you?"

"I don't know. Sometimes."

"Yes, you do. That's why you're still with me. Even if you think I'm not romantic or adventurous."

"I'm sorry I said that."

"I just wish you hadn't said it in front of the kids."

I looked back to the time clock on the Debussy piece. Seven minutes till break. I pretended to check a couple of sound meters.

"I know why you keep coming in," she said. "I'm not stupid, you know."

I knew I wasn't going to have to reply to that, so I settled back in my chair and crossed my arms, smiling at her, tilting my head.

She got out of her chair and came over behind me. She ran her hands backwards through my hair as if she were a barber, and the sensation of going against the grain was very satisfying. Her fingers felt long and hard, like bent pencils. She ran her hands back and forth over my scalp and down my neck. I groaned a couple of times. From behind she leaned over and kissed me upside down. Her tongue sprang into my mouth and explored it, licking my teeth and curling under my lips. It shot back and forth, and I tried to suck on it as hard as I could. One of her hands got under my shirt. I reached behind me and grabbed the back of her thighs just below her buttocks. Suddenly she was on my lap, pressing hard against me. I got her shirt off and was working on the pants when I heard it.

Silence.

I looked at the time clock. 00:00

"Oh Christ!" I shouted. I got her off me as quick as I could and stabbed the repeat button on the control board.

Willa giggled when I got back to the chair. Her upper chest was flush with excitement. Her bra was undone but still hanging from the bones of her shoulders. She fiddled with my zipper as I tugged her pants off. She leaned back against the table and drew me to her. We started fast but were easing off a little when the phone on the table exploded in our ears.

I stopped dead and looked at Willa.

"Keep going," she said, trying to hold my arms to her.

"But that's him," I said. "That's him."

"I know," she said. "I don't care."

The phone kept ringing at our ears. Willa reached practically behind her head and took the phone off the hook, holding it by the earpiece. A thin manic voice jabbered insistently on the other end. I thought she might be giving the phone to me and I made a reach, but she wouldn't let me have it. She looked at me, paused, and then put the phone back in the cradle. It rang again almost instantly. I unplugged the jack without picking up the receiver. Willa took her arms and drew me closer, bringing my weight on top of her as she laid back on the table. She half-groaned, and I looked into her face, her eyes, the slightly open and smiling mouth, above her lip a pink touch of smeared lipstick.

▲▲▲▲▲▲

# AMBASSADOR

▲▲▲▲▲▲▲

Allan walked over to the bar and ordered another tonic water. The Ambassador would say something if she even thought she smelled liquor on him. He took his drink and walked back through the crowded tables to take up his position at the back of the room. He passed a table of ladies talking and laughing quite loudly, and two of the ladies, both handsome and fortyish, looked at him so bluntly that he blushed and hurried by without looking back. There was a spot open along the far wall so he moved over to it and sipped his water after wiping some sweat from the bridge of his nose. He checked his watch.

Two hours later, at eleven forty-five, Allan was waiting in the black limousine when the Ambassador allowed the doorman to usher her into the plush backseat. The door closed and Allan put the car into gear. He eased his way off the grounds, into the light traffic, and east towards the haughty diplomatic turf of Rockcliffe. Snowflakes as big as butterflies flew out of the dark into the beam of the headlights.

The Ambassador was quiet, and Allan said nothing. The

radio was off, and though she did occasionally enjoy listening to soft classical music, Allan always waited for her to request it. He had been with the Consulate for ten years, nine with this Ambassador, and he still didn't know how she might react if he played different music or opened a window without asking her. He envied the easy rapport some of the other staff had with her. She did not radiate accessibility, but Allan did not seek it either.

She sneezed.

"Bless you," said Allan.

"Thank you," she said. "I believe I am contracting a cold. Oh dear." She touched her nose with a white cotton handkerchief.

The Ambassador was a petite woman. Allan had to crane his neck to look at her in the rearview mirror. "Shall I turn the heat up a little?"

"Please," she said. "There is a bite in this evening's air. I spoke to my husband this morning. He is in Colombo. He was wearing short pants and an open-necked shirt." She stopped and let Allan consider this. "Can you imagine?"

Allan laughed professionally. "No." The roads were good and he didn't think much about the weather beyond that. "How is Mr Jayachandran?" he inquired.

She took a minute to answer. "Fine, thank you. A bit under the weather lately, however. He has probably brought it on himself worrying about the political situation."

They were silent for a couple minutes until they got into Rockcliffe. Then she said, "You weren't waiting all night there for me, were you? Sitting there?"

"No."

"Were you with Julie?"

"No. She's visiting her mother on school break for a week or so."

The Ambassador was quiet for a moment. "What did you do this evening, then, if you don't think it rude of me to ask?"

"Well," he started, then hesitated. "I went to a dance."

"Oh, yes, of course, Allan. I'm sorry. You told me earlier this evening, didn't you?"

He nodded.

"And?"

He shrugged and smiled.

"Did you not enjoy yourself? Did you meet someone to dance with?"

Allan shook his head. "Not tonight."

"Enjoy yourself?"

He smiled for her. "No. Find someone to dance with."

The Ambassador smiled back at him. "That's unfortunate. You are a nice man. You will enjoy dancing when you have someone to dance with."

"It's easier that way, yes."

She was already looking out the window as he spoke. They were approaching the Consulate. Only the porch light was on, the rest of the hunched mansion dark.

"Look at that. Everyone is asleep." She tsk-tsked. "I'll have to wake somebody to have tea with me."

Allan pulled up to the front entrance and saw the Ambassador to the door, then he pulled the limousine into the heated garage. His own car was parked out behind the Consulate, and he started it before unplugging it. After letting the engine warm up for a couple of minutes, he departed.

He wondered if the dance might still be going. It was twelve-twenty. Having been to only two of these dances, and having left early both times, he didn't know how late they went. He did not want to miss anything, not access every possibility. But, then, there was another dance scheduled for next Friday. He could always go to that one.

The next dance was different almost right from the start. Twenty minutes after he arrived, a woman Allan guessed to be, like him, in her late thirties, asked him to dance. Unnerved, he found his composure just in time to accept. Her name was Beatrice. When they got to the edge of the floor the music changed. From a simple waltz to the samba.

"Uh-oh," said Beatrice. "Latin."

"Do you mind?" said Allan. They stood at the edge of the floor like scientists at the lip of a volcano.

"Well, I guess not. I'm not very good at it, but I don't care if you don't care."

"I don't care," said Allan. "I don't mind Latin music, but I can't dance to it. Not that I can dance to anything else."

Beatrice laughed. "Let's give it a shot," she said.

They plunged in, and to Allan's relief they were both bad at the samba. The song ended, and Beatrice turned to face the band, clapping enthusiastically. She wanted to stay. The next song was also Latin, so they butchered that too, but the song after that was a waltz. Beatrice accepted Allan's hand on the small of her back with a smile. It was a formal waltz and their box step was crisp, direct, uncomplicated.

Later, when they were sitting at a table with two of Beatrice's friends, they talked about the dance, the crowd, their favourite drinks. They agreed that lunch at the King Edward Hotel on Tuesday next would be nice, and convenient for both of them.

At ten fifteen Allan rose to leave. He was picking up the Ambassador at eleven.

"Well, I have to go," he said.

"Oh," she said. "All right. See you Tuesday, then."

"I'm looking forward to it."

"Me too."

He left and wasn't particularly sorry to have done so, though he was excited about Beatrice. Allan wanted things to move at his pace. Unlike life with his ex-wife, Ruth. She was now a financial planner, living in the Beaches in Toronto with another woman. He'd loved Ruth for most of their marriage, but that didn't mean much in the end, and now Allan thought of her in the same way he thought about world events—with interest, concern and the occasional personal application, but generally as something that went on without him.

The Ambassador was in a sombre mood and said little on the drive back to the Consulate. Someone who did not know the Ambassador as well as Allan might have assumed she was preoccupied with something, but when that had been the case in the past she talked freely, almost as a distraction, and her conversation at these times blinked on and off, like a flickering Christmas light.

Allan didn't mind, really, that she didn't talk, though he was surprised to find himself disappointed that she didn't inquire about the dance. He would have enjoyed telling her he had finally danced with someone, and that he was in fact having lunch with her on Tuesday.

He pulled up in front of the dark Consulate, the tires crunching on the chunky sienna gravel of the half-moon driveway. He got out to see the Ambassador to the door. The porchlight came on.

"Thank you, Allan," she said wearily, as she got out of the car. "I don't plan on needing you tomorrow, but you have the beeper in any case, don't you?"

Allan nodded.

"Good. I have something on Tuesday, but I don't think it will take too long."

"A luncheon?"

"No, no. Some after-dinner ceremony. I don't know, or care, really. I'll have the secretary phone you, in any case." They came to the door.

"That's fine," said Allan. "Good night."

"Yes. Good night."

The door opened and light spilled out. The Ambassador gingerly stepped inside. Allan glimpsed the attendant, who smiled at him. The door closed.

Allan arrived at the King Edward Hotel early enough to guarantee getting one of those overstuffed leather chairs against the far wall so that he could watch Beatrice walk in. She came into the lobby right on time, and stood in the middle of it looking around. Her long coat was unbuttoned; a beautiful deep blue skirt billowed out of it. Her short stylish hair looked messy in a purposeful way. She ran a hand through it and curled a strand behind an ear.

"Beatrice," Allan said, getting up. She smiled as he came over.

"Hello, Allan?" She didn't appear to be even remotely nervous. "How are you?"

"Fine. You?"

"Very well, thanks. Hungry just at the moment." She smiled again.

"Hey, me too," Allan said. "Let's do something about that, shall we." He ushered her to the Grill Room, off to the left of the lobby, where a coat-check girl took their coats and directed them to the reservation desk.

The maitre d' nodded as they stopped in front of him, and when he smiled bad teeth broke out from between his lips.

"Hi," said Allan. "Reservations for Kain."

They were led to a table, in the corner of the room, that seemed to be surrounded by large ferns. Allan had to brush one of them aside just to get to his seat, and long thin leaves seemed to hang over their heads when they sat down.

"I've never seen anything like this," said Allan. "I don't remember ever seeing this table."

"Probably because you couldn't," said Beatrice, looking at the plants around her.

"At least it'll be private," said Allan.

He looked from side to side, and considered getting up to ask the maitre d' for a different table. It was a nice table but, if anything, a little too private. A lot too private, actually. It would be nice to have been aware of something going on external to them. Allan felt like a zoo animal. He didn't want to be in such sharp focus just now.

"So, Allan," said Beatrice. "How have your last few days been?"

Allan looked back to her. "Oh," he said, exhaling sharply. "Umm, pretty good. Yes, quite good. Yours?"

"Not bad. I've been a little tired, lately, but nothing too serious. You know how it is. Work and everything."

Allan nodded appreciatively. A waiter suddenly appeared from an opening in the ferns.

"Good afternoon," he said. "I'm Tod. I'll be your server this afternoon. Can I start you with a drink?"

Beatrice ordered a bottle of spring water and Allan asked for a beer. The waiter quickly returned with the drinks and took their orders for lunch.

"So," Beatrice said. Allan looked attentively at her. "Did you have a good time at the dance on Friday?"

He nodded.

"I've only been to a few myself," said Beatrice. "I find them a bit intimidating."

"Really?"

"You know," she said. "I mean, it's not as if I can go out and just talk to strangers all the time."

"You're doing all right so far."

She smiled. "You know what I mean. Don't you? Don't you think its kind of hard, and a bit scary?"

"I suppose so. I've never had much luck meeting people at them."

"Really? I'd have thought you would have the women at those things all over you."

"Afraid not."

"You're just unapproachable."

"Unapproachable!?"

"Well, really, Allan. I saw you over against that wall. Cool and diffident. Who could possibly have the courage to even go talk to you."

"You did."

"Well," said Beatrice coyly. She shrugged her shoulders and batted her eyelashes.

Allan laughed. He held eye contact while he reached for his beer.

They sipped on their drinks for a few seconds. Then Beatrice straightened herself up in her chair and said, "So, what is it you do? For a living."

Allan smiled and swilled his beer around in his glass, churning up a little foam. "I'm a chauffeur."

"You're kidding!"

He shook his head. "I'm not kidding. I'm a driver with the Sri Lankan Consulate."

"Really? That's really your job?"

Allan nodded. "How about you?"

"I'm a radiologist."

Allan inclined his head. "A doctor. A radiologist, no less." He narrowed his eyes. "That's very interesting."

"Why is that interesting?"

"Well, I mean, a doctor, a radiologist. Do doctors go to dances for 'adult singles' often?"

"They do if they can't get a date." She toyed with her napkin. "Do chauffers go to adult singles dances?"

"They do if they're lonely."

The waiter burst through the ferns again, this time with their lunches. He set them down on the table. "There we go. Sole for the lady and veal for the gentleman." He clasped his hands together. "Can I get you anything else?" They shook their heads. "Right on. Enjoy."

They finished their meals more or less in silence, pausing occasionally to comment on the food. After the plates had been removed and they had coffee before them, Beatrice said, "Allan, are you going to go to the next dance? A week Friday?"

He stirred his coffee and then licked his spoon. "I don't really know. It might depend on whether I have to work."

"Will you go if you don't have to work?"

"Maybe."

"Are you divorced, Allan?"

He nodded. "You too?"

"Yes. Six years ago."

"Kids?"

"No. I always wanted to have them and he didn't. That must have had something to do with it, I suppose." She paused. "You?"

"A girl. Julie."

"Oh, how nice, Allan. I bet she's a sweet girl?"

"Yes, she's wonderful. She's twelve."

"Do you see her much?"

"Well, I've actually got custody."

"You do? Is your wife still alive?"

Allan got this all the time. "Yes. I just got custody, that's all." He took a sip of water and wiped his mouth with his napkin.

"How interesting, Allan. Tell me what happened?"

Allan took his elbows off the edge of the table and crossed his arms in front of him. He could feel his neck throbbing.

Beatrice also sat back and turned her glance on her lap for a moment. Then she looked at Allan, before picking up her coffee and taking a careful sip.

"Allan?"

"Yes?"

"Do you ever feel that things, that life, is shapeless? You know? Like fog or something?" She paused and then continued. "Like it's there all around you but there's no form. I feel that sometimes. I wish there was an outline. Something I could follow."

"A map? People with maps still get lost."

"But it would still help, I think. Don't you think? To have an idea?"

Tod, the waiter, sliced through the ferns with a bill. Allan reached for it, but Beatrice got to it first.

"No, no," said Allan. "Please, this one's on me."

"Not at all," said Beatrice. "We mutually agreed to come for lunch. I can pick up the tab if I want to."

"What if I wanted to pick up the tab?"

"Too bad. Besides, I probably make a lot more money than you." She smiled, lowered her head, and then raised her foot under the table. She dragged it a couple of inches up his shin. "Maybe I'll let you earn your keep. Soon."

An erection unfurled down Allan's pants and he felt his face and ears go red. He smiled mostly because he didn't know what else to do. "Whatever," he said, trying to sound casual but instantly regretting the stupidity of it. "Good."

Beatrice laughed then let a small furrow cross her brow.

They left the restaurant together. At the lobby door they agreed to have dinner the next week.

Allan waited until Beatrice had rounded the corner before he went back inside the hotel. He picked up a magazine in the lobby cigar shop and sat in the chair he'd sat in earlier. After flipping through his magazine for a few minutes, he closed it and indulged himself in thinking about where he and Beatrice might have their dinner, their next meeting. He reopened the magazine and spread it open over his lap.

When Allan picked up the Ambassador at ten that evening it was clear she was in a very poor mood. She exchanged no pleasantries and seemed to be uninterested in any sort of communication. It was a warm night for winter, humid and uncomfortable, with the temperature right around zero.

The Ambassador spoke just as they were coming out of downtown, nearing the river. "Allan," she said. "Why don't we cross the bridge."

"To Hull?"

"Yes, why not," she said. "We can go have a look at the Museum of Civilization."

Allan signalled left and turned onto the bridge. It was a long, low bridge, not very high above the icy Ottawa River. The tires made bumping sounds as they crossed. When they reached the Quebec shore, Allan again signalled left and they were there, almost on top of the huge swooping lines of the Museum.

"Pull up over there," said the Ambassador, pointing to a parking lot across the street. "I want to be able to get a perspective."

Allan kept the car running while they sat and looked at it.

"It is so massive," said the Ambassador. "So beautiful." She sounded still and composed. Allan could hear her breathing. He looked back out to the building. It had a strange and unsettling power, with its awesome rolling outline, like a dream of liquid prairie hills, surging across landscapes, making them its own.

"Can we return now, Allan," said the Ambassador, after about five minutes. "I am really very tired."

Allan pulled out of the parking lot and got back onto the bridge. He'd decided earlier he was going to tell the Ambassador about Beatrice, even if she didn't ask.

"I'm having dinner with a lady next week," he said. "Would you like me to tell you about her?"

The Ambassador did not respond right away. "I spoke to my husband today," she finally said. "He is not that well."

"I'm sorry to hear that, " said Allan, feeling a little put off. "I hope he's feeling better soon."

"Allan," she said. "He is very ill. He will not live long."

"What?" Allan said softly.

"Yes."

She looked out the window and sighed heavily. "Allan?" she asked him softly.

He drove, slowly, quietly. "Yes?"

"My feelings for my husband. They must help him? In some way?"

Allan was quiet for a moment. "I think they have to," he said. "Somehow."

It was becoming a blustery night. As they came off the bridge the backlighting of downtown outlined the Parliament buildings against the sky, calling to mind a lonely vision of a distant jagged sierra.

"You know, Allan, I have loved him greatly. That is everything, isn't it?"

Allan pulled off the bridge and headed left, towards the Consulate. Traffic was non-existent, the black road glistened like a wet seam of coal. A light rain began to fall, more a mist than actual drops. He nudged the wiper switch and the long rubber blades began moving silently across the windshield. After a brief shoulder check Allan signalled and changed lanes, and picked up his speed a little. He glanced in his rear-view mirror. The Ambassador was looking at him, her eyes wide beneath her pulled-back black hair, her thumb and forefinger pinching her lips closed. Allan looked at her for as long as he could, before he had to return his gaze to the road.

▲▲▲▲▲▲

# NEW ROPE

Against Vivian's advice, Ellison made plans to visit his older brother on the west coast. Darryl had phoned exactly one week after Ellison convocated, and invited him out to Red Point Lodge, the resort at which he was Head Golf Professional.

"I don't think you should go," Vivian had said when they discussed it over dinner. "I really don't. He didn't come out here for your convocation after you made a point of asking him." She sat with her arms on the table, tapping her fingernails on the wooden surface. Her long red hair fell off her shoulders across her face; she swept it back behind her ears. Ellison found her very attractive, except when she was telling him what to do. "I mean, why *should* you go visit him?" she concluded.

In truth, Ellison had had similar thoughts, but didn't say so to Vivian. "It's not that big a deal," he said. "I'm sure he had good reasons for not coming."

If Darryl did have "good" reasons, or any reasons at all, Ellison did not know what they were. Darryl simply hadn't said whether he was coming or not, and then he just didn't show up on the day. But although he was angry with Darryl, Ellison didn't want to say no to him just out of spite. That wasn't the kind of thing he saw himself doing.

Vivian splashed some red wine into her glass and took a large swig. A tadpole of wine swam down the bowl to the stem when she set it back on the table. "I think he's selfish, Ben. You know that, too. Don't apologize for him." The lips of her large expressive mouth looked pale and bloodless, even when she bunched them up toward her nose.

Ellison picked up her glass and dabbed his napkin at the stem. "I'm not apologizing for him. I'm just going to see him, that's all." He set the glass back down in front of her and picked up his own. "Don't make a thing out of it."

"Whatever you say." Vivian took her arms off the table and crossed them under her breasts, increasing her cleavage, making her breasts seem heavier and fuller than they actually were. "But I am right," she said.

When Ellison checked in for his flight to Vancouver, the woman helping him took the large black bag containing his golf clubs and sent them down the luggage chute. Darryl had insisted Ellison bring his clubs, though now, at the airport, Ellison thought how much easier it would have been to just borrow some from Darryl. He was not really sure he wanted to play golf, or, more fundamentally, if he even liked the game. At least it took four or five hours to play a round. That would eat up considerable time.

"You lucky devil," said the ticket woman as she crisply stapled his baggage ticket to his boarding pass.

Ellison raised his eyes from her hands to her face.

"Off for a little golf holiday?" she continued. She was about fifty years old and looked active and healthy, the kind of woman who might golf and ski with her family.

"No," he said. It had never occurred to him to think of this trip as a holiday.

The woman said, "Oh," looking at him quizzically.

He forced out a smile for her. "Well, sort of a golf holiday, I guess" he said. "Kind of a family visit. We might play some golf."

She smiled back, less warmly than before, and handed him his boarding pass. "Have a good trip."

Ellison took a cab from the airport to the Horseshoe Bay Ferry Terminal. It was an enormously long drive from south of the city to north of it, a taxi ride that actually took longer than the flight from Edmonton and cost nearly the same. He just made the ferry leaving for Nanaimo. After having to sprint for it, he sat in an exhausted heap as the boat churned away from the dock.

Stupid golf clubs, he thought, shaking his head. Lurching and scampering down the gangway with his suitcase and clubs, he imagined he must have looked like some hunchback fleeing a mob with a small body tucked in his armpit. When the ferry docked, after a short and impossibly scenic trip across the Strait of Georgia, Ellison looked in the parking lot. No Darryl.

It was a lovely quiet day, sylvan and warm. He lugged his stuff to the edge of the lot, pulled out his paper, sat on his suitcase, and waited.

Fifteen minutes later a van pulled into the lot. It was an old Volkswagen with the fold-up sleeping quarters; these were partially extended, and made the vehicle look like something Rommel might have driven in North Africa. The VW circled the north side of the parking lot, a bull in a ring. It stopped, idled, turned and began driving straight at Ellison. It wasn't moving that fast, but it wasn't exactly inching forward either. Ellison tensed up. The driver was stoned, maniacal, had had a heart attack. Ellison looked to his left, his right. There was a fence behind him. He dropped his paper, did a little stutter step, and got ready to leap but the driver hit the brakes and pulled the van sharply to the right.

"Christ Almighty!" he exclaimed, feeling hot blood sprinting throat to temple.

"Ben!" said the driver, a woman. "Are you Ben Ellison?"

"Yes!!" he said. "What were you doing? Driving at me like that!?"

She revved the engine. "Oh, that's just the brakes. Sometimes you've got to stand on them."

Ellison nodded slowly.

"I'm Melody," she said. "Darryl was in the middle of a lesson and asked me to come get you. Hop in." She looked to be in her late twenties. Her hair was long and straight, dirty blonde; one strand down the right side had coloured string wound tightly around it. A gold stud the size of a small pea poked through the left nostril of her beakish nose.

Ellison tossed his luggage in the back of the van and went to the passenger side. The seat had been removed, and in its place was a lawn chair.

"You want me to sit in this?" asked Ellison. "Are you serious?"

"It's tied down," she said. "Besides, I drive slow. Don't drive with Darryl, though, man. He thinks he's Jackie Stewart." She burst out laughing and then broke into a slurring impersonation of an angry Scot. She didn't look at Ellison until she stopped, at which point she smiled charmingly for him, showing a mouthful of white niblet-sized teeth.

Melody kept her eyes on the road as she drove, and true to her word she held the van's speed to a fraction of the posted limit. Whenever the empty highway deviated even slightly to the right or the left she signaled. The engine was whining in second gear.

"Are you Darryl's partner?" Ellison asked her.

"Partner!?" she half-sneered. She looked briefly at him, then turned her eyes back to the road. "Are you asking me if we're sleeping together?"

"No," he said, frowning a little. "It's just that Darryl's never mentioned you or anything."

"What a coincidence!" she said. "Until last week he never mentioned you either."

After ten minutes of silent driving, they pulled off the highway at a sign that said Red Point Lodge and Golf Club. They continued briefly down the road, past a canola field on the left and the sea on the right. Soon they were inside the boundary of the golf course; it was lush and green, and some of the holes crossed over the road. The routing of the course took it inland and seaside. Melody slowed down.

"Boy, this looks beautiful."

"Thank you," said Melody.

Ellison paused. Thank you? "What hole is this right here?" he said after a minute.

Melody shrugged. "Number 8, I think."

"You're not sure?"

"I don't golf."

"You don't golf?"

She looked slyly at Ellison. "You're still trying to figure out if your brother is fucking me, aren't you?" She was still smiling, but readjusted her gaze as though she were assessing him. "I see what he meant?"

"What do you mean, 'What he meant'?"

She ignored him and pulled the van into a parking spot assigned to the Head Professional.

"So do you work here?" asked Ellison.

She nodded. "Owner."

"Owner? Really?"

She gave him a sharp look. "Is there a problem with that?"

"No, no," said Ellison hurriedly, feeling his ears go hot. "No, I think it's great. But, you're young-looking, that's all. That's why I sound a little surprised. I mean, sorry I insulted you."

Melody started to giggle as she turned off the van. "Hey, relax. Don't have a cardio." She opened her door. "Darryl's over on the range. You could go over there if you want. He wouldn't mind."

Ellison extricated himself from the lawn chair. As he did so, the chair sprang shut like a leg hold trap. Leaving it flat on the floor, he got out of the van, locked the door, and looked, unsuccessfully, for a knob to roll up the window. Melody was already halfway up the stairs leading into the lodge, a huge log structure that looked like an old yet elegant mountain chalet, and Ellison scrambled after her.

"The practice range is out behind the pro shop," she pointed. "And the lounge is just in here. Whatever you have while you're here, just charge it to your room. It's taken care of."

He stood in the foyer and watched as she walked down a side hallway that led to a cluster of administrative offices. The lounge was a high-ceilinged room done in mountain lodge style, with log walls, central stone pillars and a large fan rotating lazily above. A stone fireplace dominated one end of the room. The mounted head of an elk hung over the mantle.

He left the lounge and went over to the practice range. Even from a distance, he could make out his brother's burly shape. He was standing with a taller, thinner man. When Ellison got nearer, Darryl waved and pointed to the chairs directly behind the practice area. Ellison sat down at a deck table with a big umbrella sketching out a pool of shade.

"Easy jobs don't make the money, Darryl," the man was saying. "It's the hard jobs that make the money. Sales is hard work. I mean, look at Gandhi. Why did he succeed? Because he had a target. Four things, okay. One, pack and unpack a box correctly. That's key. Two, find people to sell to. Don't forget, Gandhi had a great market. Three, present the product in its best light. And four," he said, pausing meaningfully, "you must know how to properly fill out a sales order form."

Darryl nodded sympathetically.

"You'd be great at it. There's a lot of money in tile. Just look at my Dad."

"That's good of you to say, Al. See you next week."

Al put his clubs in his bag, said goodbye and went off in the direction of the clubhouse. Ellison got up and went over to where Darryl was standing.

"I think tile is for you, Darryl. I really do."

Darryl started to laugh, but held it since Al was still not yet inside the clubhouse. "So how are you, man?" he said after a moment.

"Fine. Except Melody nearly ran me over in the parking lot."

They both laughed and Darryl said, "How's work?"

Ellison stiffened. "Work?"

Darryl picked up a golf club and wiped the face of it with a damp filthy cloth rag. "I mean, school. You're done now, right?"

"Convocated a month ago. I invited you. Remember?"

"Yeah," said Darryl. "Sorry I couldn't make that. Late spring is always brutal around here."

"No problem," said Ellison, looking off in the direction of the clubhouse and lodge.

Darryl replaced the club in his bag. "So you want to grab a drink and get caught up, or you want to wait until dinner. We got time over the next few days. I want you to ree-lax." He gave Ellison a warm smile.

"Maybe a rest," he said. "That might be good."

They went back to the van, got Ellison's luggage and went to his room, agreeing to meet at five p.m. in the lounge for a drink before dinner. After Darryl had gone, Ellison explored his room. The bedroom was large and had a well-appointed bathroom with a whirlpool tub. There was a small galley kitchen and a huge living area with a chunky red sofa and two teal wingback reclining chairs. A television sat in the corner, near a door leading to a balcony which looked out on to the golf course. From this spot Ellison could see to the horizon, which was dotted with clumpy little islands sitting in the blue silent Strait of Georgia.

"Unbelievable," he said to the empty room.

He realized he was suddenly thinking about Darryl in a different light. This place was where his brother worked. In a significant position. How had Darryl managed this, to live and work in such surroundings? By playing golf?

At five, Ellison went down to the main lounge. Darryl was near the fireplace, sitting with Melody and another man, who stood up as Ellison approached.

"Ben," said Darryl. "This is Angus Wilson, the assistant pro."

They shook hands and Angus said hello in a thick guttural Scottish accent. After one drink they moved to the dining room, ate, and then returned to the same seats they had occupied earlier, circling the hissing and spitting fire. The room was a bit warm, but very comfortable, and Ellison spent a long time talking to Angus, asking him about where he'd grown up (Aberdeen), what course he played as a kid (Cruden Bay), and why he'd moved to Canada (for love).

"Love!" said Ellison. "Really?"

"She were from Vancouver," said Angus, who'd been drinking heavily all through dinner, and was now starting to talk slow. "Couldn't live without the garl."

"She's dead," said Melody matter-of-factly. "Cracked her nut open diving into the pool twelve years ago. I was fifteen. I remember it like it was a picture on the wall. Angus was off playing a tournament in Portland. Trudy was her name. A big swan dive into the shallow end. Kee-runch. Pretty stupid thing to do actually. My dad tried to revive her, but it was over like that."

Angus lowered his head. Ellison thought at first this was a moment of personal reflection, and bent his head in kind. After a second, he looked up and saw that Angus was picking an insect out of his scotch glass. When he got the bug out, he flicked it off his finger onto the floor. "Gnat," he said solemnly, slowly raising the glass back to his lips.

"He's still in denial," said Melody.

"Hey," said Darryl. "I haven't asked yet. How's Vivian?" He swilled back the last of a rum and coke and chewed on an ice cube.

"Fine," said Ellison.

"Still a bitch?" asked Darryl, chuckling, looking into his glass for another ice cube.

Ellison scowled, put down his glass and uncrossed his legs. His skin was hot from being so close to the fire. He rubbed his forearm and the coarse hairs felt brittle from the dry heat.

Darryl fidgeted for a second, before Melody cut in. "That's your girlfriend, I take it," she said to Ellison. "Oh, sorry," she smiled slyly. "I mean, 'partner'."

Ellison stared half-lidded at her, trying to suppress a smile.

She stuck out her tongue at him, and as she did so Ellison noticed she was wearing a scantily applied, but still apparent, touch of plum-coloured lipstick. She also seemed to have a better tan than Ellison remembered.

"Hey," said Darryl "I was just kidding, Ben. Really."

"What a kidder," said Melody.

"I like Vivian. She's just a little uptight. I mean, you've got to admit."

Ellison said nothing for a moment. He picked up his drink. "At least *she* was at my convocation. At least she cared enough to show up."

Darryl sat and looked at Ellison. "Well, why would I want to go something like that, anyway?" he said pleadingly. "I didn't even think you were serious. I mean, Jesus."

"It does sound a great fucking bore," said Angus from deep in his chair, putting heavy emphasis on the profanity.

"That's hardly the point," said Ellison. "You're my brother."

"Hey," said Melody. "Let's go out to the pier for a while. It's such a great night."

"Fucking straight up," slurred Angus. He rose from his chair and immediately collapsed into a squat, like a baby failing in an attempt to stand. Darryl stood up and helped him to his feet. They got to the van and began pulling out of the parking lot. Suddenly Angus emerged from his nearly vegetative state of drunkenness. "Wait!" he shouted at the top of his lungs. "Stop!"

Darryl hit the brakes. "What? What, for fuck's sake?"

Angus opened his door and staggered over to his car. He groped himself for a minute or two before locating his keys. After dropping them two or three times, he got the trunk open and looked to be pulling out a tree stump, but it was his golf clubs. After placing them carefully on the ground, he slammed the trunk hard on his left hand.

"Argghhh!" he shouted. Everyone piled out of the van and went over. He was on the ground with his legs out in front of him. Melody gently probed at his hand.

"None of the fingers are broken," she said. "It looks like he closed the trunk across the top."

Angus was groaning and holding his right hand over his eyes.

"Let's get him in the van," said Melody.

They hauled Angus into the back of the van, where he lay down and went to sleep.

"Grab his clubs anyway," said Darryl to Ellison. "We'll use those."

The pier was a few miles down the coastline. They had to drive inland, along the highway, then back out to the ocean. Even so, the drive took no more than ten minutes. Darryl pulled the van up close to the foot of the pier, which ran out to sea off a kind of high retaining wall. They all got out. At the foot of the pier, there was a drop of ten feet to the water, which lapped weakly on the thin beach. The length of the pier ran off into the darkness. A light mist hung weightless in the air and somewhere far away a horn sounded longingly.

Melody came up beside Darryl. "What do you want to do with Angus?" she said.

"Let him sleep."

They walked out onto the pier, carrying Angus's golf clubs. When they reached the end they sat down and dangled their legs off the last plank. The drop to the water was about thirty feet. The ocean was so still and dark and calm it might have been solid earth.

Ellison looked back and saw Angus's clubs, and said, to no one in particular, "I don't like golf."

"No kidding," said Melody, who laid back on the pier, and placed her hands flat out beside her body. "It's just for fat white people," she continued. "Thank God they've got money, that's all I have to say."

Ellison was looking at Melody, nodding, and was about to add to what she'd said when Darryl broke in.

"They've got to have something to do, don't they? Everybody deserves a pastime. You guys are being snobs. You just don't understand the game, so you're making fun of it."

They sat quietly for a few moments, before Darryl reached into his pocket and pulled out a joint. He lit the dope and passed it to Melody. She took a drag and passed it to Ellison who took it and had a couple of deep drags.

"Hey," said Melody to Ellison. "What did you say you did your thing in, your whatchamacallit?"

"Ph.D. In Comparative Literature."

Melody yawned, gape-mouthed, for what seemed minutes and then she turned to Ellison. "Jesus, sorry."

"I think it's pretty impressive," said Darryl, in a supportive voice. "I think it's great."

"Absolutely," said Melody, hiccuping. "Literature compared to what, though?"

Ellison paused. "The literature of various languages and cultures studied comparatively."

Melody turned her sober look from Ellison to Darryl and then broke into a giggle. She put one open-fingered hand over her face and held the other arm straight in the air, palm out, as though she was asking for permission to go to the bathroom. "Sorry," she spluttered. "Sorry."

"Don't be such a bag," said Darryl.

"Well, what about you then?" Ellison said to Melody. "How did you end up owner of the Red Point Lodge and Golf Resort for fat rich white people?"

Melody took her hand off her face and stretched both arms behind her, leaning back. She was wearing a thin top and when she arched backwards Ellison saw she wasn't wearing a bra. She had small breasts, but her nipples were big and had gotten hard, which made the light cotton shift tent out around them.

Darryl, sitting cross-legged, said, "Do you want me to tell it?"

Melody shook her head. "My dad owned it," she said. "He bought the land. Always dreamed of something like this, to get out of sales. He was in tile."

Ellison turned to Darryl, who pointed at Melody. "Brother."

"Al. Anyway, Dad made a shitload of money. Millions with franchising and everything. So he bought the land. Got Robert Dye Thompson III to do the design. Opened the course to rave reviews. Played one year and then dropped stone cold dead, croaked, heart attack. On the sixth hole."

"My goodness," said Ellison. "So what about Al?"

"Are you saying he'd make a better owner than me?"

"No," said Ellison hurriedly. "Jesus Christ, you're sensitive."

"Well, think about what you're saying."

They fell into another silence until Darryl stood up, took a club from Angus' bag, carefully placed a ball on the surface of the pier, and then whacked it into the night. There was a quiet splash in the distance.

Melody watched Darryl impassively. "There's a metal buoy about two hundred yards straight out," she said.

Ellison looked out but couldn't see anything.

"I know exactly where it is," said Darryl. "I like shooting for it at night, because then it's all feel and intuition. I have to be happy with myself, though. Usually a little drunk. I've never hit it when I'm uptight." He stared out in the direction of the buoy. "When I just let it happen, it happens. But I have trouble letting go. Whenever I really want to hit it, when I think about hitting it, I miss."

Darryl placed another ball on the pier and launched it, holding his end-of-swing posture until there was another muted splash.

"Almost," said Melody. She had her eyes closed. "I'd say no more than five feet."

"How many times have you hit it?" Ellison asked.

Darryl shrugged. "Six, maybe seven times."

"You should see Angus," said Melody.

"He can do it at will," said Darryl. "He's got the magic move. Right here." Darryl demonstrated a certain position of the hands at the top of the swing.

"Too bad he's passed out," said Melody.

"Here," said Darryl, handing the club to Ellison. "Give it a shot."

"No," said Ellison. "I don't think so."

Melody made an exasperated hissing exhalation. "For fuck's sake," she said. "Just stand up and do it, will you. It's not a test."

Ellison stood up.

"Just don't think about it," said Darryl. He placed a ball on the pier and held out the club. Ellison took it. He looked off in the direction of the buoy, and felt a strange kind of pressure. Not to hit the buoy, of course, but a different kind of pressure. What was it exactly he wasn't supposed to think about?

He took a couple of easy warm-up swings, addressed the ball, and then swung back slowly, trying hard not to think of the ball, the buoy, the water, the club, anything. He swung down sharply and clipped the top of the ball. It skittered off the edge of the pier and plopped into the water. The golf club, at the moment just past impact, twisted in his hand, then slipped completely out of his grip as he followed through. It helicoptered through the mist and dark, and splashed into the ocean, making a considerably noisier entry than the ball.

"Oh, shit!" he said.

Melody looked at Darryl as she bolted upright, holding her stomach. "That was great!" she said. "That's hilarious!"

"Oh my God, Darryl, I'm sorry," said Ellison.

Darryl stood, hands on hips, looking forlornly at the spot where the club had entered the water.

"Forget the ball," laughed Melody. "The *club* almost made it to the buoy!"

"I'm giving you a lesson tomorrow," said Darryl.

Ellison grimaced. "It wasn't a special club, was it? Was it an heirloom?"

"No," said Darryl, still downcast.

Melody laughed from deep in her stomach. "Even I've never thrown the club in the ocean!"

"I hardly meant to."

Darryl picked up the clubs. "We should head back," he said. "We should have the clubs in the van before Angus wakes up." He turned and began walking back down the pier. Melody followed him, still laughing. Ellison looked back into the ocean. The ripples were no longer visible. The club was gone. He couldn't remember, wondered if he even ever knew, what he wasn't supposed to think about.

The next day, early in the afternoon, Ellison was at the practice range watching Darryl. The facility was empty except for the two of them. Little pyramids of balls were stacked every five or ten yards, waiting for golfers to come along and bring the fragile structures down. Darryl stood out in the sun, swinging.

Ellison sat in the shade and didn't really start watching his brother until he'd been there ten minutes. But in the heat, under a big deck umbrella, with a drink at his side, and the time and leisure to watch, he could see that there was very much an artful purpose to the movements Darryl made. It was action and reaction. Engaging in a considered and complex motion so as to produce a desired result.

Melody came out of the lodge in the distance. She started walking over to the practice range. Ellison followed her all the way. Her hips swivelled as she walked, not so much sensually as athletically, as if she were loosening up for a distance race. She was wearing sunglasses and looked like the French women he remembered from Paris; jaunty, confident.

"How's your drink?" she asked, when she arrived at his chair.

"Good," he said, looking at his beer. "Thanks."

She looked at Darryl. "He's good, isn't he? I mean, is he? He looks like he's good."

"He can do what he wants with it."

Melody looked at Ellison and spoke behind cover of her hand, "It sure doesn't look that hard."

"I just cannot believe you've never played," Ellison snorted. "For heaven's sake, Melody, you own a golf resort. Haven't you ever even been tempted to take the game up?"

She sat back in her chair and considered Ellison through her sunglasses. "It's not that freaky, you know. Lots of people don't play golf."

"Not people that own golf resorts."

"Anyway, look, I didn't come over here to watch Darryl practice." She leaned closer to Ellison. "I need to talk to you."

"Sure." He pulled his chair nearer hers.

She motioned at Darryl. "Meet me out on the pier, tonight. You know, where we went last night. Say, eleven."

"How am I going to get there?"

"Here," she said, handing Ellison a key. "It's for Darryl's jeep. He's always in bed by ten."

She stood up, went over to Darryl, chatted for a second, and then left. Ellison watched her all the way back to the lodge.

"Hey!" said Darryl. He'd stopped and was laughing at Ellison.

"You'll see her again. Don't worry."

"No, no," said Ellison, blushing. "No, I was just thinking about something."

"I'm sure you were," said Darryl, still chuckling. "Anyway, come on up here. I'll try to give you a quick lesson, then maybe we can go play."

Ellison got up and went over to where his brother stood. He strode into an area outlined with what looked like body chalk.

"Hey! HEY!" said Darryl, shooing Ellison back. "What're you doing?"

"What?" said Ellison, hopping backwards. "You told me to come over."

"Not through that," he said. "That's ground under repair. You're not supposed to walk on that."

"Why?"

Darryl made exasperated sounds. "It's distressed turf. Can't you see that?"

Ellison looked at the ground. The grass was a bit sparse, but it hardly looked distressed. A little ignored perhaps, but he would never have even noticed it if it hadn't been pointed out to him. He moved around the area and went over to where his brother stood waiting for him.

When Ellison got to the pier later that night, Melody was waiting for him, sitting in the same place from which he'd sent Angus's club to its watery grave. She was wearing the same clothes she'd been wearing the night before. Ellison sat down beside her.

"Tide's in," said Melody. "I don't like it when the tide is in. It feels crowded. Angus feels like that, too. He only shoots for the buoy when the tide is out."

"How was he today?"

Melody shrugged. "Like every other day."

"Did his wife really die like that? In the pool?"

"Sort of," she said. "The pool was empty. Figure it out."

Ellison stared at the wood planks of the pier.

"What about you?" continued Melody. "Darryl tells me you're going to get married. To Vivian." She said Vivian like she was learning a new word.

"Could happen."

"Was what Darryl said about her the truth? That she's a bitch."

Ellison was silent for a second. "Darryl's just that way because he senses she doesn't like him."

"What's not to like?"

Ellison cocked his head and looked at Melody. "Are you guys together?"

Melody leaned back much like she had the night before. "I don't think so," she said, locking her eyes on Ellison's.

"No?"

"We had our thing." She looked up into the sky. "What's it like? That's what I want to know. Being with someone forever."

"It's not such a bad feeling."

"But think about it. You'll be fucking the same woman for the rest of your life. If you're faithful. I mean, that's great and all. But, for instance, you would never have the chance to even think that you might end up fucking someone like me." She was looking in the direction of the buoy.

"It doesn't mean a person doesn't think about stuff like that."

"A person?"

"Don't you think you're putting a little too much emphasis on sex?"

"Is Vivian pretty?" asked Melody.

"Yeah, I think she genuinely is," he said. "I think most people would say that."

"Boy, you've really got to convince yourself about that."

Ellison suddenly remembered her words in the van the other day. "What did you mean, when you said you saw what Darryl meant about me? What did he say about me?"

"He told me lots about you."

"Like what?"

Melody had stretched out on the dock and taken her sandals off. "He said you liked to know things. That knowing things, knowing things about other people, made you feel like you had control over your own life."

"He said that?"

Melody sat up. "You don't give Darryl much credit do you?"

"How do you mean?"

"You're so patronizing. Like what you just said. 'He said that?' Why did you react like that? Because you're surprised Darryl would say something insightful, something that sounds like the kind of thing you might say. That's pretty condescending, you know."

Ellison sat looking out at the ocean. The moon was mirroring off the still water and the whole looked like a wobbly sand timer.

He laid back on the pier and could hear Melody breathing beside him. It was slow and assured, deep breaths, like she was concentrating on it. She moved, slid closer to him, then sat cross-legged and put his head in her lap. She put her hand to his face, touched his chin, his forehead, stroked the area between his nose and upper lip. "You're not quite as good looking as Darryl said you were," she said. "Not bad, though."

"Thanks a lot," said Ellison

She bent over and kissed him along the scalp line. She kept her hand in his hair near the top of his ear and tilted her head to look at him. "I'm going to head on back, I think. You going to stay? Or do you want to head back?" She paused. "What do you think?"

"I might sit here a little longer," said Ellison.

Melody stood up, touched the side of his head and said quietly, "Whenever." Then she started back down the pier.

Ellison watched her go. At the foot of the pier she turned and waved. Ellison couldn't quite see her face, but he waved back, and then she was gone.

He sat looking at the sea like a person enraptured before a painting. He'd never heard the ocean so quiet. The stillness of it completely confounded his prairie understanding of the sea as a thing to be fearful of. It was marvellously calm, a sensation enhanced by the shortened horizon brought on by the darkness. He felt a kind of giddy peace. The ocean was nothing to be afraid of.

Ellison became conscious of a sound. A motor. The noise was faint but approaching, a sputtering. Who would be out in a boat at this time of night? Suddenly an idea struck him. He would phone Vivian early the next morning and ask her to come out for the weekend. She would enjoy it, and besides, she needed to get to know Darryl better.

The reality, though, despite his sudden idea, was that she might not come. This was a possibility. Actually, it was a probability. He laughed, tilted his head back, and spat off the end of the pier, enjoying the freeness of doing it, of seeing the gob disappear into the dark and the ocean. Maybe he wouldn't phone her. Whether she came or not, Ellison decided to stay a little longer. Darryl would like that. Melody wouldn't mind him taking up a room for a few more days. He thought of Melody. He hadn't heard her car start up. Ellison thought of her leaning back, braless. He imagined what it would be like to suck on one of her nipples, gently, insistently. He closed his eyes and his tongue went to the small circle of his lips.

The sputter of the boat engine was drawing closer. He peered into the dark. There was definitely something coming in. The sound grew and soon a small craft began to emerge from the black. It was a short skiff, sail down, mast up like a candle in a slice of cake. The boat bobbed into the pier. Ellison wasn't sure if the person at the rudder could see him, but he waved anyway and said hello. There was no response. The person cut the motor and drifted alongside. Suddenly a coil of rope clonked down at Ellison's feet, startling him. He picked up the length of twine. It was new rope, thin, but strong and supple. There was a ready made loop at the end, which he attached to a knob on the pier. He stood at the edge and squinted back down, saw shapes, forms, and wondered if there was anything else he was supposed to do.

▲▲▲▲▲▲▲

# THE COFFIN

▲▲▲▲▲▲▲

**O**n January 4, 1960, the French philosopher and novelist Albert Camus died in a car crash on the way from Lourmarins to Paris. January 4, 1960, was also the day, so I'm told, that my parents conceived me in Calgary, Alberta. I was made aware of this coincidence around the age of eighteen by my paternal grandfather, Neil, whom I lived with in Edmonton after the death of my father.

"What do you make of that?" Neil asked me when he told me about the coincidence. "Strange, isn't it?"

I was just another kid who didn't want to go to university, though, because of Neil's urging, I did read philosophy. I didn't mind philosophy, but I wanted to be a woodworker.

"That's pretty cool," I said. "Was he cool?"

"He most certainly was," said Neil. "French, good-looking and dynamite with the ladies."

"All right," I said approvingly.

I lived with Neil for eleven years. My parents died in separate car accidents, and I was in the car on both occasions. My mother died when I was nine, my father when I was thirteen. Both crashes left me unscathed, physically, and emotionally I have healed as much as I am going to. The only visible holdover is that I do not drive. But this is largely at the insistence of Neil, who pretends to believe that I am the incarnation of the spirit of Albert Camus.

Neil was a natural with wood, though he earned his paycheck teaching philosophy at the University of Alberta, and it was from him that I learned the beautiful symmetry of working with wood. I also learned from him that philosophy and woodworking are just different sides of the same coin. Both are about construction, about imagination interwoven with system. The rendering of elements into a coherent structure. There is a design at the heart of everything, Neil used to say, whether with oak or knowledge or people. The artist is the person who can find it. I believed him to be right and earn my living as a woodworker today.

One evening my wife came out to the garage, which I have converted into a woodworking studio. It was about ten thirty, past our bedtime, but we had just returned from visiting at the hospital and I had gone straight out to the garage. She came in, bringing the cool fall air with her, and stood by the door, considering my latest project, the pieces of which I had up on a waist-high 8'x2' trestle. She was looking, not talking. Just watching me work the palm sander. I saw her and turned it off, propped my safety glasses on my forehead.

"Honey," she said. "Don't you think it's just a bit morbid?"

I put the sander down. "Neil wants to be buried. In a coffin. I'm making it."

She kept watching me, her arms wrapped around her ribs. "Does Neil know? Have you told him, I mean? That you're building him a coffin?"

"No," I said. "It hasn't exactly come up."

Neil had been admitted to Oncology at the University of Alberta Hospital the previous week. The doctors had said he'd go soon, that his thoracic cancer was inoperable and would eat him from the inside out. The doctors also told us that we should prepare for him to die at any moment, and they told us this as if it is a kind of preparation we have been schooled in.

Anne kicked at some sawdust on the floor. "Do you want a ride to work tomorrow?"

"I'm taking the day off," I said. "I'm going to spend the morning with Neil and come back here in the afternoon."

"Oh," Anne said. "I can give you a ride to the hospital, then."

"Sure."

I knew I was being a little uncommunicative, but I was anxious to get back to work on the coffin. I picked up the sander. It was going to be a beautiful piece. Simple yet elegant. Solid mahogany. I was going to stain it with a light oil to highlight the long smooth grain, which had the pattern of soft waves emanating from a disturbance at the centre of a still pond.

I looked back to Anne. "Are you going to stand there all night?"

"I was saying a prayer for Neil."

"Oh."

"What about you?" she said.

"Prayers?"

"No, are you going to stay here all night?"

"No," I said. "I just want to finish this section."

She nodded. "I'll make some tea."

"Sure." I turned on the sander and its whine precluded further conversation. I put my safety glasses back on and went back to the piece I was edging.


Neil and my grandma had a good relationship. I understood this as a kid, just by being around them, but Neil talked a lot about Grandma after she died. They had a lot of fun together, he said, and even though they argued a lot, about anything, there was always an element of play to it, as if they were just teasing each other and knew it. I do remember sitting at our kitchen table when my own parents were still alive, listening to the four of them talk. Neil, my father's father, was logical, wordy and secular; Grandma was common sense, tell-tale facial gestures and deeply Catholic.

Neil became a much more serious man after Grandma died. Every November thereafter, on the anniversary of her death, he carved or built out of wood, crucifixes and little churches and once even the Tablet of the Ten Commandments. Every year it was something different. Grandma had always wanted him to convert, but he never did. The making of these things was his apology.

Anne took me to the hospital the next day on her way to work. I went to Oncology, but they had moved Neil to Intensive Care. When I got to ICU, there were different visitor-entrance criteria, and it took me ten minutes just to get through the doors and then into his room, which he was sharing with one other patient. When I walked in there were three doctors standing over Neil's bed. I went and stood at the edge of the group.

"You must be David," said one of the doctors. I said I was and they introduced themselves. They were all young, which bothered me immediately. They didn't look much older than myself.

Neil was conscious. He was lying on his back with tubes up his nose and an IV needle in his arm. I smiled at him and he gave me a feeble nod.

"Why has he been moved from Oncology?" I asked, still looking at Neil. I ran my hand over his hair and forehead.

The doctor who was obviously in charge didn't look at me, only at Neil. "Well," he said, in a cheerful voice, "we just thought it would be nice for Neil here to have a change of scenery. Isn't it better here, Neil?"

Neil's mouth was open, trying to breathe as best he could, so he didn't say anything, but he looked at the doctor and moved his head deliberately from side to side. The three doctors laughed heartily.

"No lack of spirit," said the one in charge. "We like having you anyway, Neil." He patted Neil on the leg. They made a show of closing some flip charts they had in their hands, and started towards the door. I followed them out into the hallway.

"We moved him late last night," said the main doctor, half to me and half to the other doctors. "He's got a bad infection, maybe pneumonia. We're pretty sure he aspirated some vomit at some point last night."

"Which means?"

"Which means that he's going to have a tougher time than he would have already. I'll be honest, he could be in for a rough ride."

I looked at the three of them in turn. "He knows he's going to die," I said. "Please don't be so condescending to him next time."

I went back into the room. Neil had his eyes closed but opened them when I said his name. I put my face close to his. His breath was wretched and he had blobs of mucous in the corners of his eyes which I cleaned out for him. He needed a shave. He closed his eyes again when he knew I wasn't going to leave right away.

"Hey, Neil," I said softly. "How're they treating you here?"

He took a deep breath and spoke as he exhaled. "Same as other place," he hissed.

"That bad, eh?"

He nodded. We sat in silence for a couple of minutes. He opened his mouth like he was going to speak, so I put my face closer.

"I'm old, aren't I, David?" he said. "Eighty-two, you know." He said it as if no one else knew.

I smiled at him. "Yes, I know, Neil. You're an old coot."

"An old coot," he laughed and hissed air out. "That's right." He stopped laughing and fixed his look at me though he kept his eyes closed. "We don't die, you know, David. Did you know that?

We don't."

"Why's that?" I asked.

He let his eyes open. "Better to die on one's feet than live on one's knees. Camus said that."

"I know," I said, smiling. "I haven't forgotten."

"You're not driving are you, Albert?"

"No," I said, somewhat taken aback. I couldn't tell if he was joking.

He looked at me then as if he suddenly did not know me. He closed his eyes and appeared to fall into a sleep. A moment later a nurse bustled noisily into the room, and his eyes flashed open at her like klieg lights. He looked terrified and he shut them again right away. After a couple of minutes he drifted into a very restless sleep, moaning loudly, muttering about his head, his stomach. I spoke to the nurse and she gave him a Tylenol injection, which calmed him slightly. I sat at his bed and watched him for the next three hours. Occasionally he said something in his sleep, saying somebody's name. Once he lifted his arm and went through the motions of writing something, a letter perhaps.

Sitting there I thought that my life, from this point forward, would be well spent directly emulating him. He was a kind and thoughtful man who lived his life with integrity. A man whose legacy ought to be having people emulate him.

I left the hospital around lunchtime and spent the afternoon working on Neil's coffin. When Anne got home she saw where I was and came out.

"How's Neil?" she asked.

I leaned on the trestle. "He's not so great," I said. "Not making a lot of sense. They've moved him to ICU."

She didn't say anything but stepped forward and ran her hand over one of the corner pieces of the coffin, then all the way down the edge to where I was standing. She lightly touched other parts of the coffin, then sifted her fingers through my hair and patted it down. "I know how much you want to give him something," she said softly. "I'm going to go see him after dinner. Will you come with me?"

I ran my sleeve over my eyes and nodded.

"Good," she said. She looked at the coffin and then me, as if she were going to say something about it but changed her mind. She kissed me and went back to the house.

After dinner I collected some shaving material so that I could give Neil a shave that evening. At the hospital I got a bowl of hot water and a couple of towels. Anne helped me put the foam on his face and he tried to joke with us, but it cost him a lot of energy so he stayed quiet.

"Here we go, Neil," I said, as I drew the blade down from his sideburns to his chin. I took a few more strokes and then had to stop for a minute, my hands were shaking so bad.

"Are you all right?" Anne whispered.

I bent my head forward. Neil had heard Anne.

"Don't nick me," he said, air whistling lightly out from between his teeth.

Anne and I smiled. She leaned over and gave him a kiss on the temple. "You hear everything, don't you?" she said. He gave one nod.

We finished shaving and rinsing him, and then I put some aftershave on him. He turned his mouth down as best he could. "I smell funny," he whispered. Then he tried to smile. He was in obvious pain, and Anne went to get a nurse to give another injection.

When Anne left the room I bent close to him.

"Neil," I said into his ear. "Neil, can you understand me for a few minutes." I drew my head back and looked back at him. He didn't say or move anything but he opened his eyes and squinted hard at me, as if to fight the pain.

"Neil, I've made you something."

He kept looking, his eyes were starting to water and he wasn't blinking.

"I got some beautiful mahogany. Gorgeous panels." I stopped for a second. "I'm just finishing it and I wanted to tell you."

I began to describe it to him and he closed his eyes. He looked asleep but he kept his arm up the whole time, placing his palm against my chin and cheek, then gently rubbing it over my face, touching my ears. Once or twice he made a small little fist and lightly tapped me on the chin. I held on to his other hand.

He never said a word until I stopped. He closed his eyes and took a breath. He barely got it out, and only did because it was an exhalation. It was too faint to hear, but it didn't matter. I knew what he was saying. I was certain I would never again feel the way I felt at that moment, that I could not ever again feel anything so much. I would have traded him places if I could have.

Anne returned with a nurse who was carrying a tray full of bottles and needles and cotton swabs. The nurse gave him an injection, but it didn't seem to do him any good. He moaned and moved his head from side to side. He kept trying to roll over, but couldn't.

A nurse came in at about ten o'clock. "You can probably go, you know," she said kindly. "He's been like this every night. Not that that's a comfort, I know, but you won't do yourselves much good sitting here. Go have a good sleep."

Anne thanked her and then talked me into leaving.

Neil and Anne had been fond of one another from the first time they'd met and were fast friends even before it was clear that Anne and I were going to stay together and be serious. I think that they would have stayed friends even had Anne and I not gone on to get married. Neil was like the proud father at the wedding, and Anne asked him to give the Toast to the Bride, at which he did a magnificent job.

"Tell me something else about your wife," Anne always asked

Neil whenever there was a lull in the conversation. At first she asked out of politeness, but later out of interest and respect.

"Well, Anne," Neil would say. "She was funny. That's the best thing I remember about her. She was really funny." Then he would tell an anecdote or two, and the way he told them always did make us laugh. The one thing he always told Anne was how much she was like Grandma. When Anne and I fought he usually took her side; he would listen to me afterwards and then tell me I should be more considerate of her.

"You should thank your lucky stars you have someone like that. There are billions of unhappy people out there."

Anne's parents lived in Toronto, and she only saw them on holidays, though she talked to them on the phone regularly. But Neil, she always said, was her resident father.

We got a call early the next morning, and the nurse asked us to come in as soon as we could because Neil was struggling. On the drive over we were mostly silent.

"Are you okay, David?" Anne asked at one point. "For what might happen?"

I didn't respond. I was holding the shoulder strap of the seat belt with both hands, zinging it in and out of the slot. We took 114 Street, the main road heading north to the hospital and the university. I watched the morning traffic and people waiting at bus stops. The sun had just come up on our right, and it followed us to the hospital like a big yellow eye.

When we got to the hospital Anne dropped me off at the Emergency door and went to park the car. I walked slowly to ICU and on the way to Neil's room passed a couple of nurses who offered me cheerful good mornings.

There was a nurse in Neil's room who was doing something to one of the tubes in his nose. She looked up when I came in and acknowledged me, but didn't offer any other sort of greeting.

"What's happening," I said.

She spoke as she worked, taping a tube over his nostril. "He's not doing so hot. His coma score dropped badly overnight."

"Coma score?"

"Indicators," she said, not looking at me. "Predictors."

I looked at him lying on the bed. He was unconscious and he looked visibly worse than when we'd left him the night before. His skin had no colour and his forehead was clammy to the touch, feverish but cold.

"He's dying," I said to the nurse. "Is he dying?"

She looked at me directly but didn't say anything one way or the other. Anne came in and saw me.

"The doctor," said the nurse, "is on the way." She turned and left the room.

Anne went over to Neil and stroked his forehead. "Oh, Neil," she said. She took a deep breath. "Oh, poor Neil."

A doctor arrived a few minutes later, not the main doctor but a junior one, and told us that Neil was going to die that day, that if he didn't it would be both a miracle and a curse, since he would only deteriorate.

"You don't have to stay in the room, if you don't want to. Many people don't," he said. "He will have staff around him all the time and it might be easier for you."

I said nothing and looked at the floor the whole time he spoke. It was up to us, he said, and obviously we could stay in the room if we wanted.

We went back into the room, and it wasn't more than fifteen minutes later that Neil had a spasm and lunged for breath, held it, and then coughed up a mouthful of mucous. He lunged again and this time his breathing stopped altogether. It started again after a few seconds. Anne and I were beside him on either side of the bed. She held him and I had my palms flat lightly across his chest.

He was completely comatose now, no longer able to feel pain, operating only on the orders of his central nervous system. Every breath was harder than the last, and each one diminished him as if he were a sandcastle going under a slow tide. Anne held him and whispered to him, "We love you, Neil. You know that. We all love you. David and me. We won't ever stop."

Neil didn't breathe when he should have, then started again in a different pattern. The veins in his throat were throbbing wildly.

"Anne," I said, quietly. "I...I can't. Oh, Jesus."

"Go," she said, turning her head towards me, but still holding Neil in her arms. "It's okay. I'm here with him."

She turned back to Neil and started whispering to him again, with her head right by his ear. He stopped and started breathing. I could hear strands of mucous bubbling in his throat when he struggled for air.

I went out into the hallway, sat on a plain metal chair and held my head. My mind ran from thought to thought, finding reason or solace in none of them. A few minutes later two nurses went into the room together and re-emerged almost immediately, one of them going one way down the hall and the other the opposite way.

Sitting upright in the hard metal chair, I saw my white knuckles gripping the armrests. People milled about the hallway, going in this room, leaving that one. A family was gathered in discussion with a doctor outside the room next to Neil's. Better to die on one's feet than live on one's knees, Camus had said. It sounded hollow, and possibly even untrue.

I was no longer conscious of time or my surroundings and did not know how much later it was that Anne came out, found me in the chair, touched my head. It might have been hours. She let me sit for a moment longer and then asked if I wanted to go home.

## Acknowledgements

Many people have provided me with support and timely interventions. For these things, I want to thank Barb Broda, Dave Maloney, Pat Chemago, Liz Barker, Paul Matwychuk, Wendy Hollo, Janet Pavlic, Mgsr. Bill Irwin, Dusten Stewart, Steve Janzen, John Kelly, Sean McDermott, Charlotte McKay, Steven Heighton, Randy Kohan, Susan Skaret, Barb and Murray Fraser, Laura Kugler, Phil Lawson (who is dearly missed) and his family, Eileen, Caroline and Elizabeth.

I'd also like to thank some friends whose part in this book is bigger than they will ever know: Rich Haigh, Charlotte Davis, Murray Rode, and Bruce Grierson. Similarly, I am in great debt to Trevor Ferguson and Greg Hollingshead. A thank you is meagre repayment for what these friends have given me. I also want to thank Barbara Sapergia and Geoffrey Ursell for their care and attention.

Some of the stories in this collection were written during time provided to me by the Alberta Foundation for the Arts. Thank you to the staff and juries of the AFA. Thanks also to *The Malahat Review, Quarry, The Fiddlehead,* and *Prairie Fire,* which published some of these stories in earlier versions.

Finally, there are three women I want to recognize. My mother and grandmother taught me much, including why reading is so important. And my wife Cathy has a level of grace, humour and intelligence that makes her both inspiring and easy to be with. Thank you to all three.

**C**urtis Gillespie has lived most of his life in Calgary and Edmonton. His fiction has appeared in the Coteau anthology *Stag Line*, and in a number of literary periodicals, including *Quarry*, *The Fiddlehead*, *The Malahat Review*, and *Prairie Fire*. This is his first book.